Elsie in the South

The Original Elsie Classics

Elsie Dinsmore

Elsie's Holidays at Roselands

Elsie's Girlhood

Elsie's Womanhood

Elsie's Motherhood

Elsie's Children

Elsie's Widowhood

Grandmother Elsie

Elsie's New Relations

Elsie at Nantucket

The Two Elsies

Elsie's Kith and Kin

Elsie's Friends at Woodburn

Christmas with Grandma Elsie

Elsie and the Raymonds

Elsie Yachting with the Raymonds

Elsie's Vacation

Elsie at Viamede

Elsie at Ion

Elsie at the World's Fair

Elsie's Journey on Inland Waters

Elsie at Home

Elsie on the Hudson

Elsie in the South

Elsie's Young Folks

Elsie's Winter Trip

Elsie and Her Loved Ones

Elsie and Her Namesakes

Elsie in the South

Book Twenty-Four of
The Original Elsie Classics

Martha Finley

CUMBERLAND HOUSE
NASHVILLE, TENNESSEE

Elsie in the South
by Martha Finley

Any unique characteristics of this edition:
Copyright © 2001 by Cumberland House Publishing, Inc.

Published by Cumberland House Publishing, Inc.,
431 Harding Industrial Drive, Nashville, Tennessee 37211.

Cover design by Bruce Gore, Gore Studios, Inc.
Photography by Dean Dixon Photography
Hair and Makeup by Calene Rader
Text design by Heather Armstrong

Printed in the United States of America
1 2 3 4 5 6 7 8 – 05 04 03 02 01

CHAPTER FIRST

"WHAT A STORM! There will be no going out today even for the early stroll about the grounds with papa," sighed Lucilla Raymond one December morning, as she lay for a moment listening to the dash of rain and sleet against her bedroom windows. "Ah, well! I must not fret, knowing Who appoints the changes of the seasons, and that all He does is for the best," her thoughts ran on. "Besides, what pleasures we can all have within doors in this sweetest of homes and with the dearest and kindest of fathers!"

With that, she left her bed and began the duties of dressing, first softly closing the communicating door between her own and her sister's sleeping apartments lest she should disturb Gracie's slumbers, then turning on the electric light in both bedroom and bathroom, for, though after six, it was still dark.

The clock on the mantel struck seven before she was quite through with these early morning duties, but the storm had in no wise abated in violence. As she heard it, she felt sure that outdoor exercise was entirely out of the question.

"And I'll not see Chester today," she sighed half aloud. "It was evident when he was here last night that he had taken a cold, and I hope he won't think of venturing out in such weather as this."

Just then the door into Gracie's room opened, and her sweet voice said, "Good morning, Lu. As usual, you are up and dressed before your lazy younger sister has even begun the duties of dressing."

"Take care what you say, young woman," laughed Lucilla, facing round upon her. "I am not going to have my delicate younger sister slandered in that fashion. She is much too feeble to leave her bed at the early hour which suits her older and stronger sister."

"Very kind of you to see it in that light," laughed Gracie. "But I must make haste now with my dressing. Papa may be coming in directly, for it is certainly much too stormy for him and you to take your usual stroll in the grounds."

"It certainly is," assented Lu. "Just listen to the hail and rain dashing against the windows. And there comes papa now," she added, as a tap was heard at their sitting room door.

She ran to open it and receive the fatherly caress that always accompanied his morning greeting to each one of his children.

"Gracie is not up yet?" he said inquiringly, as he took possession of an easy chair.

"Yes, papa, but she is not dressed yet. So, I shall have you all to myself for a little while," returned Lu in a cheery tone, seating herself on an ottoman at his knee.

"A great privilege," he said with a smile, passing a hand caressingly over her hair as he spoke. "It is storming hard. You and I must do without our usual early exercise about the grounds."

"Yes, sir. And I am sorry to miss it, though a chat with my father here and now is not so bad an exchange for it."

"I think we usually have that along with the walk," he said, smiling down into the eyes that were gazing lovingly up into his.

"Yes, sir, so we do. But you always manage to make the shut-in days very enjoyable."

"It is what I wish to do. Lessons can go on as usual with you and Gracie as well as with the younger ones, and after that we can have reading, music, and quiet games."

"And Gracie and I have some pretty fancy work to do for Christmas gifts."

"Ah, yes! And I presume you will both be glad to have a little—or good deal—of extra money with which to purchase gifts or materials for making your gifts."

"If you feel quite able to spare it, father," she returned with a pleased smile. "But not if it will make you feel in the least cramped for what you want to spend yourself."

"I can easily spare you each a hundred dollars," he said in a cheery tone. "Will that be enough, do you think?"

"Oh, I shall feel rich!" she exclaimed. "How very good, kind, and liberal you are to us and all your children, papa."

"And fortunate in being able to be liberal to my dear ones. There is no greater pleasure than that of gratifying them in all right and reasonable desires. I think that as soon as the weather is suitable for a visit to the city we will take a trip there for a day's shopping. Have you and Gracie decided upon any particular articles that you would like to give?"

"We have been doing some bits of fancy work, father, and making up some warm clothing for the old folks and children among our poor neighbors.

We have also purchased a few things for our house servants. And to let you into a secret," she added with a smile and a blush, "I am embroidering some handkerchiefs for Chester."

"Ah, that is right!" he said. "Chester will value a bit of your handiwork more than anything else that you could bestow upon him."

"Except perhaps the hand itself," she returned with a low, gleeful laugh.

"But that he knows he cannot have for some time," her father said, taking in his the one resting on the arm of his chair. "This one belongs to me at present, and it is my fixed purpose to hold it in possession for at least some months to come."

"Yes, sir. I know that and highly approve of your intention. Please never give up your claim to your eldest daughter so long as we both live."

"No, daughter, nothing is further from my thoughts," he said with a smile that was full of obvious affection.

"What do you want from Santa Claus, my dear papa?" she asked.

"Really, I have not considered that question," he laughed. "But anything my daughters choose to give me will be highly appreciated."

"It is pleasant to know that, father dear. Now please tell me what you think would be advisable to get for Mamma Vi, Elsie, and Ned."

That question was under discussion for some time, and the conclusion was arrived at that it could not be decided until their visit to the city stores to see what might be offered there. Then Gracie joined them, exchanged greetings and caresses with her father, and as the call to breakfast came at that moment, the three went down together, meeting Violet and the younger children on the way.

They were a cheerful party, all at the table seeming to enjoy their meal and chatting pleasantly as they ate. Much of their talk was of the approaching Christmas and what gifts would be appropriate for different ones and likely to prove acceptable.

"Can't we send presents to brother Max, papa?" asked Ned.

"Hardly, I think," was the reply. "But we can give him some when he comes home next month."

"And he'll miss all the good times the rest of us have. It's just too bad!" replied Ned.

"We will try to have some more good times when he is with us," said the captain cheerily.

"Oh, so we can!" was Neddie's glad response.

The captain and the young people spent the morning in the schoolroom as usual. In the afternoon, Dr. Conly called. "I came in principally on your account, Lu," he said, when greetings had been exchanged. "Chester has taken a rather severe cold so that I, as his physician, have ordered him to keep within doors for the present, which he deeply regrets because it cuts him off from his daily visits here."

"Oh, is he very ill?" she asked, vainly trying to make her tones quite calm and indifferent.

"Oh, no! Only in danger of becoming so unless he takes very good care of himself."

"And you will see to it that he does so, Cousin Arthur?" Violet said in her usual sprightly tone.

"Yes, so far as I can," returned the doctor with a smile back at his cousin. "My patients, unfortunately, are not always careful to obey orders."

"When they don't, the doctor cannot be justly blamed for any failure to recover," returned the captain. "But I trust Chester will show himself docile and obedient."

"Which I dare say he will if Lu sides strongly with the doctor," Gracie remarked, giving Lucilla an arch look and smile.

"My influence, if I have any, shall be on that side," was Lucilla's quiet rejoinder. "He and I might have a bit of chat over the telephone, if he is able to go to it."

"Able enough for that," said the doctor. "But he is too hoarse, I think, to make himself intelligible. However, you can talk to him, bidding him be careful and for your sake to follow the doctor's strict directions."

"Of course I shall do that," she returned laughingly. "Surely he will not venture to disregard my orders."

"Not while he is liable to be sent adrift by his lady-love," said Violet in sportive tone.

Just than the telephone bell rang, and the captain and Lulu hastened to it.

It proved to be Mrs. Dinsmore of the Oaks, who called to them with a message from Chester to his affianced—a kindly greeting, a hope that she and all the family were well, and an expression of keen regret that he was, and probably would be for some days, unable to pay his accustomed visit to Woodburn.

"There, daughter, take your place and reply as you deem fit," said Captain Raymond, stepping aside from the instrument.

Lucilla at once availed herself of the permission.

"Aunt Sue," she replied, "please tell Chester we are all very sorry for his illness, but we hope he may soon be well. We think he will if he is very careful to follow the doctor's directions. And when this storm is over, probably some of us will call at the Oaks to inquire concerning his welfare."

A moment's silence, then came the reply. "Chester says, thank you. He will be glad to see any or all of the Woodburn people, but you must not venture out till the storm is over."

"We won't," returned Lucilla. "Good-bye." And she and her father returned to the parlor where they had left the others with their report of the call.

Two stormy days followed. Then came one that was bright and clear, and they gladly availed themselves of the opportunity to go to the city, do their Christmas shopping, and call at the Oaks on their return. They reached home tired but in excellent spirits, having been very successful in making their purchases. They found Chester recovering from his cold.

From that day until Christmas time, the ladies and little girls of the connection were very busy in preparing gifts for their dear ones, Grandma Elsie as well as the rest. She did not come so often to Woodburn as was her custom, and the visits she did make were short and hurried.

Chester was a frequent caller after recovering from his cold. Even while he was there, Lucilla worked busily with her needle, though never upon the gift intended for him. She now wore and highly prized a beautiful diamond ring that he had given her in token of their betrothal, though she had told him at the time of its bestowal that she feared it had cost more than he could well afford. At which he laughed, telling her that nothing could be too good or expensive for one so lovely and charming as herself.

"In your partial eyes," she returned with a smile. "Ah, it is very true that love is blind. Oh, Chester, I often wonder what you ever found to fancy in me!"

In reply to that, he went over quite a list of the attractive qualities he had discovered in her.

"Ah," she laughed, "you are not blind to my perhaps imaginary good qualities but see them through multiplying glasses, which is certainly very kind of you. But, oh, dear! I'm afraid you'll find out your mistake one of these days!"

"Don't be disturbed. I'll risk it," he laughed. Then added more seriously, "Oh, Lu, darling, I think I'm a wonderfully fortunate fellow in regard to the matter of my suit for your heart and hand."

"I wish you may never see cause to change your mind, you dear boy!" she said, glad tears springing to her eyes. "But, ah, me! I fear you will when you know me better."

"Ah," he said teasingly, "considering our long and rather intimate acquaintance, I think you are not giving me credit for any great amount of discernment, Lulu."

"Well," she laughed, "with regard to my faults and failings probably the less you have of that the better for me."

They were alone in the library, and the house was very quiet, most of the family having already retired to their sleeping rooms.

Presently Captain Raymond came in, saying with his pleasant smile, "I should be sorry to seem inhospitable, Chester, but it is growing late. I am loath to have my daughter lose her beauty sleep. Please don't for a moment think I want to hurry you away from Woodburn, though. The room you occupied during your illness is at your service, and you are a most welcome guest."

"Many thanks, captain. But I think I should go back to the Oaks at once lest someone should be waiting up for me. I should have brought my night key, but I neglected to do so," Chester replied, and in a few minutes he took leave.

The captain secured the door after him and turned to Lucilla, saying, "Now, daughter, you may bid me goodnight and make prompt preparations for bed."

"Oh, papa, let me stay five minutes with you," she entreated. "See, I have something to show you," holding out her hand in a way to display Chester's gift to advantage.

Her father took her hand in his. "An engagement ring!" he said with a smile. "A very handsome one it is. Well, dear child, I hope it may always have most pleasant associations to you."

"I should enjoy it more if I were quite sure Chester could well afford it," she said with a sigh.

"Don't let that trouble you," said her father. "Chester is doing very well, and probably your father will be able to give some assistance to you and him at the beginning of your career as a married couple. Should Providence spare me my present income, my dear eldest daughter shall not be a portionless bride."

"Papa, you are very, very good to me!" she exclaimed with emotion. "You are the very dearest of fathers! I can hardly bear to think of living away from you, even though it may not be miles distant."

"Dear child," he said, drawing her into his arms, "I do not intend it shall be even one mile. My plan is to build a house for you and Chester right here on the estate, over yonder in the grove. Some day in the near future, we three will go together and select the exact spot."

"Oh, papa, what a delightful idea!" she exclaimed, looking up into his face with eyes dancing with pleasure. "Then I may hope to see almost as much of you as I do now, living in the same house."

"Yes, daughter mine. That is why I want to have your home so near. Now bid me goodnight and get to your bed with all speed," he concluded with a tender caress.

❧❦❧❦❧❦❧❦

CHAPTER SECOND

"THEY ARE GOING to have a Christmas tree at Ion, one at Fairview, one at Roselands, and I suppose one at the Oaks," remarked Ned Raymond one morning at the breakfast table. "But I guess folks think Elsie and I have grown too old for such things," he added with a tone of melancholy resignation and with a slight sigh.

"A very sensible conclusion, my son," said the captain cheerfully with a twinkle of amusement in his eye. "But now that you have grown so manly, you can enjoy more than ever giving to others. The presents you have bought for your little cousins can be sent to be put on their trees, those for the poor to the schoolhouses, and if you choose you can be there to see the pleasure with which they are received. Remember what the Bible says, 'It is more blessed to give than to receive.'"

"Oh, yes, so it is!" cried the little fellow, his face brightening very much. "I do like to give presents and see how pleased folks look that get them."

"And as papa is so very liberal to all of us in the matter of pocket money, we can every one of us have that pleasure," said Gracie.

"Yes, and I know we're going to," laughed Ned. "We didn't go so many times to the city and stay so long there for nothing. And I don't believe grandma and papa and mamma did either."

"No," said his mother. "I don't believe anybody — children, friend, relative, servant, or neighbor — will find himself neglected. And I am inclined to think the gifts will be enjoyed even if we have no tree."

"Oh, yes, mamma! And I'm glad to be the big fellow that I am, even if it does make me have to give up some of the fun I had when I was small," Ned remarked with an air of satisfaction.

"And tonight will be Christmas Eve, won't it, papa?" asked Elsie.

"Yes, daughter. Some of us will be going this afternoon to trim the tree in the schoolhouse. Do you, Elsie and Ned, want to be of the party?"

"Oh, yes, sir! Yes, indeed!" was the joyous answering exclamation of both.

Then Elsie asked, "Are you going, mamma? Sisters Lu and Gracie, too?" glancing inquiringly at them.

All three replied that they would like to go, but they had some work to finish at home.

A part of that work was the trimming of their own tree, which was brought in and set up after the departure of the captain, Elsie, and Ned for the schoolhouse.

Violet's brothers, Harold and Herbert, came in and gave their assistance as they had done some years before when Max, Lucilla, and Gracie had been the helpers of their father at the schoolhouse. The young girls had enjoyed that, but this was even better, as those for whom its fruits were intended were nearer and dearer. They had a merry, happy time embellishing the tree with many ornaments and hanging here and there mysterious pachages, each carefully wrapped and labeled with the name of its intended recipient.

"There!" said Violet at length, stepping back a little and taking a satisfied survey. "I think we have finished at last."

"Not quite," said Harold. "But you and the girls may please retire while Herbert and I attend to some small commissions of our good brother—the captain."

"Ah! I was not aware that he had given you any," laughed Violet. "But come, girls, we will slip away and leave them to their own devices."

"I am entirely willing to do so," returned Lucilla merrily, following in her wake as she left the room.

"I, too," said Gracie, hastening after them, "for one never loses by falling in with papa's plans."

"What is it, Harold?" asked Herbert. "The captain has not let me into his secret."

"Only that his gifts to them all—his wife and daughters—are in the closet and are to be taken out now and added to the fruits of this wondrous tree," replied Harold, taking a key from his pocket and unlocking a closet door.

"Ah! Something sizable, I should say," laughed Herbert, as four very large pasteboard boxes came into view.

"Yes. What do you suppose they contain?" returned his brother, as they drew them out. "Ah, this top one—somewhat smaller than the others—bears little Elsie's name, I see. The other three must be for Vi, Lu, and Gracie. Probably they are new cloaks or some sort of wraps."

"Altogether likely," assented Herbert. "Well, when they are opened in the course of the evening, we shall see how good a guess we have made. And here," taking a little package from his pocket, "is something Chester committed to my care as his Christmas gift to his betrothed."

"Ah! Do you know what it is?"

"Not I," laughed Herbert. "Though a great deal smaller than her father's present, it may be worth more in regard to monetary value."

"Yes, and possibly more as regards the giver, even though Lu is evidently exceedingly fond of her father."

"Yes, indeed! As all his children are and have abundant reason to be."

Herbert hung the small package on a high branch, then said, "These large boxes we will pile at the foot of the tree — Vi's at the bottom, Elsie's at the top, the other two in between."

"A very good arrangement," assented Herbert, assisting him.

"There, we have quite finished, and I feel pretty well satisfied with the result of our labors," said Harold, stepping a little away from the tree and scanning it critically from top to bottom.

"Yes," assented Herbert. "It is about as attractive a Christmas tree as I ever saw. It is nearing teatime now, and the captain and the children will doubtless soon return. I think I shall accept his and Vi's invitation to stay to that meal. Will you not?"

"Yes, if no call comes for my services elsewhere." And with that they went out, Harold locking the door and putting the key into his pocket.

They found the ladies in one of the parlors and chatted there with them until the Woodburn carriage was seen coming up the drive. It drew up before the door and presently Elsie and Ned came bounding in, merry and full of talk about all they had done and seen at the schoolhouse.

"We had just got all the things on the tree when the folks began to come," Elsie said. "Mamma, it was nice to see how glad they were to get their presents! I heard one little girl say to another, 'this is the purtiest bag, with the purtiest candy and the biggest orange I ever seed.' And the one she was talking to said, 'Yes, and so's mine. And aint these just the goodest cakes!' After that they each—each of the girls in the school I mean—had two pair of warm stockings and a woolen dress given to them, and they went wild with delight."

"Yes, and the boys were just as pleased with their coats and shoes," said Ned. "The old folks, too, with what they got, I guess. I heard some of them thank papa and say he was a good, kind gentleman."

"As we all think," said Violet with a pleased smile. "But come upstairs with me now. For it is almost tea time, and you need to be made neat for your appearance at the table."

They were a merry party at the tea table and enjoyed their fare but did not linger long. On leaving the table, Violet led the way to the room where she, her brothers, Lucilla, and Gracie had been so busy. Harold produced they key and threw the door open, giving all a view of the Christmas tree and its tempting fruits and glittering ornaments.

Ned, giving a shout of delight, rushed in to take a nearer view, Elsie following close in his wake, the older ones not far behind her. Christine, having another key to the door had been there before them and lighted up the room and the tree so that it could be seen to the very best advantage.

"Oh, what a pile of big, big boxes!" exclaimed Elsie. "And there's my name on the top one! Oh, papa, may I open it?"

His reply was a smile as he threw off the lid and lifted out a handsome astrakhan fur coat.

"Oh! Oh!," she cried. "Is it for me, papa?"

"If it fits you," he replied. "Let me help you to try it on." He suited the action to the word, while Harold lifted the box and pointing to the next one, said, "This seems to be yours, Gracie. Shall I lift the lid for you?"

"Oh, yes, if you please," she cried. "Oh! Oh! One for me, too! Oh, how lovely!" as another astrakhan fur coat came to light.

He put it about her shoulders while Herbert lifted away that box and, pointing to the address on the next, asked Lucilla if he should open that for her.

"Yes, indeed! If you please," she answered, her eyes shining with pleasure.

He did so at once, bringing to light a handsome sealskin coat. "Oh, how lovely! How lovely!" she exclaimed, examining it critically. "Papa, thank you ever so much!"

"You are heartily welcome, daughters, both of you," he said, for Gracie, too, was pouring out her thanks, her lovely blue eyes sparkling with delight.

And now Violet's box yielded up it's treasure—a mate to Lu's—and she joined the young girls in their thanks to the giver and expressions of great appreciation of the gift.

"Here, Lu, I see this bears your name," said Harold, taking a small package from the tree and handing it to her.

She took it, opened it, and held up to view a beautiful gold chain and locket. As she opened the latter, "From Chester," she said with a blush and smile. "Oh, what a good likeness!"

"His own?" asked Violet. "Ah, yes! And a most excellent one," she added, as Lucilla held it out for her inspection.

"Oh, here's another big bundle!" exclaimed Ned. "With your name, mamma, on it! And it's from grandma. See!" pointing to the label.

"Let me open it for you, my dear wife," said the captain and doing so brought to light a tablecloth and dozen napkins of the finest damask with Violet's initials beautifully embroidered in the corner of each.

"Oh, they are lovely!" she said with a look of delight. "They are worth twice as much for having such specimens of mamma's work upon them. I know of nothing she could have given me which I would have prized more highly."

There was still more—a great deal more fruit upon that wonderful tree. There were various games, books, and toys for the children of the family and the servants, suitable gifts for the parents of the latter, useful and handsome articles for Christine and Alma, and small remembrances for different members of the family from both relatives and friends.

Chester joined them before the distribution was quite over, and he was highly pleased with his share, especially the handkerchiefs embroidered by the deft fingers of his betrothed.

The captain, too, seemed greatly pleased with his as well as with various other gifts from his wife, children, and friends.

The distribution over, Violet's brothers hastened to Ion to go through a similar scene there. And much the same thing was in progress at the homes of each of the other families of the connection.

Grandma Elsie's gift to each daughter, including Zoe, was similar to that given to Violet—tablecloth and napkins of finest damask, embroidered by her own hand with the initials of the recipient. Each was a most acceptable present to each.

Ned had received a number of very gratifying presents and considered himself as having fared well, but Christmas morning brought him a glad surprise. When breakfast and family worship were over, his father called him to the outer door and, pointing to a handsome pony grazing near at hand, said in his pleasant tones, "There is a gift from Captain Raymond to his youngest son. What do you think of it, my boy?"

"Oh, papa," cried the little fellow, clapping his hands joyously. "Thank you, thank you! It's just the very best present you could have thought of for me! He's a little beauty, and I'll be just as good to him as I know how to be."

"I hope so, indeed," said his father. "And if you wish you may ride him over to Ion this morning."

"Oh, yes, papa! But mayn't I ride him about here a while just now, so as to be sure I'll know how to manage him on the road?"

"Why, yes. I think that's a good idea, but first you must put on your overcoat and cap. The air is too cool for a ride without them."

"Oh, mamma and sisters!" cried Ned, turning about to find them standing near as most interested spectators. "Haven't I got just the finest of all the Christmas gifts from papa?"

"The very best for you, I think, sonny boy," returned his mother, giving him a hug and kiss.

"And we are all very glad for you, my dear little brother," said Gracie.

"I as well as the rest, dear Ned," added Elsie, her eyes shining with pleasure.

"And we expect you to prove yourself a brave and gallant horseman, very kind and affectionate to your small steed," added Lucilla, looking with loving appreciation into the glad, young face.

"Yes, indeed, I do mean to be ever so good to him," rejoined the little lad, rushing to the hat stand and, with his mother's help, hastily assuming his overcoat and cap. "I'm all ready, papa," he shouted the next moment, racing out to the veranda where the captain was giving directions to a servant.

"Yes, my son, and so shall I be when I have slipped on my coat and cap," returned his father, taking them with a smile of approval from Lucilla, who had just brought them.

The next half hour passed very delightfully to little Ned, learning under his father's instruction to manage skillfully his small steed. Having had some lessons before in the riding and management of a pony, he succeeded so well that, to his extreme satisfaction, he was allowed to ride it to Ion and exhibit his Christmas gift there, where its beauty and his horsemanship were commented upon and admired to his heart's content.

The entire connection was invited to take Christmas dinner at Ion, and when they gathered about the table not one was missing. Everybody seemed in excellent spirits, and all were well, excepting Chester, who had a troublesome cough.

"I don't quite like that cough, Chester," said Dr. Conly at length. "And if you asked me for a prescription, it will be a trip to Florida."

"Thank you, Cousin Art," returned Chester with a smile. "That would be most agreeable if I could spare the time and take with me all of the present company, or even a part of it."

"Meaning Lu, I presume, Ches," laughed Zoe.

"Among the rest. She is one of the present company," he returned pleasantly.

"What do you say, captain, to taking your family down there for a few weeks?" asked Dr. Conley, adding, "I don't think it would be a bad thing for Gracie, either."

"I should have no objection if any of my family need it, or if they all wish to go," said the captain, looking at his wife and older daughters as he spoke.

"A visit to Florida would be something new and very pleasant, I think," said Violet.

"As I do, papa," said Gracie. "Thank you kindly for recommending it for me, Cousin Arthur," she added, giving him a pleased smile.

"Being very healthy, I do not believe I need it, but I should greatly enjoy going with those who do," said Lucilla, adding in an aside to Chester, who sat next to her. "I do hope you can go and get rid of that trying cough."

"Perhaps after a while. But not just yet," was his low-toned reply. "I hardly know what I should like better, Lu."

"Well, don't let business hinder. Your life and health are of far more importance than that, or anything else."

His only answer to that was a smile that spoke appreciation of her solicitude for him.

No more was said on the subject just then, but it was talked over later in the evening and quite a number of those present seemed taken with a desire to spend a part of the winter in Florida. Chester admitted that by the last of January he could probably go without sacrificing the interests of his clients, and the captain remarked that by that time Max would be at home and could go with them.

Grandma Elsie, her father and his wife, and Cousin Ronald and Annis pledged themselves to be of the party, and so many of the younger people hoped they might be able to join that it bade fair to be a large one.

"Are we going in our yacht, papa?" asked Ned.

"Some of us, perhaps, but it is unfortunately not large enough to hold us all comfortably," was the amused reply.

"Not by all means," said Dr. Conly. "The journey can be taken more quickly by rail and probably more safely at this time of the year."

Their plans were not matured before separating for the night, but it seemed altogether probable that quite a large company from that connection would visit Florida before the winter was over. At the Woodburn breakfast the next morning, the captain in reply to some questions in regard to the history of that State, suggested that they, the family, should take up that study as a preparation for their extended visit there.

"I will procure the needed books," he said, "and distribute them among you older ones to be read at convenient times during the day and reported upon when we are all together in the evenings."

"An excellent idea, my dear," said Violet. "I think we will all enjoy it. I know that Florida's history is an interesting one."

"Were you ever there, papa?" asked Elsie.

"Yes. I found it a lovely place to visit at the right time of the year."

"That means the winter time, I suppose?"

"Yes, we should find it far too unpleasantly warm in the summer."

"How soon are we going, papa?" asked Ned.

"Probably about the first of February."

"To stay long?"

"That will depend largely upon how we enjoy ourselves while there."

"The study of the history of Florida will be very interesting, I am sure, father," said Lucilla. "But we will hardly find time for it until next week."

"No," he replied. "I suppose not until after New Year's—as we are to go through quite a round of family reunions. But in the meantime, I will, as I said, procure the needed books."

"And shall we learn lessons from them in school time, papa?" asked Ned.

"No, son, when we are alone together in the evenings or have with us only those who care to have a share in learning all they can about Florida. Our readers may then take turns in telling the interesting facts they have learned from the books. Do you all like the plan?"

All thought they should like it. So it was decided to carry it out.

That week was indeed filled with a round of most enjoyable family festivities, now at the home of one part of the connection, now at another, and wound up with a New Year's dinner at Woodburn. There was a good deal of talk among them about Florida and the pleasure probably to be found in visiting it that winter—to say nothing of the benefit to the health of certain of their company, Chester especially, as he still had a troublesome cough.

"You should go by all means, Chester," said Dr. Conly, "and the sooner the better."

"I think I can arrange to go by the first of February," replied Chester. "And I shall be glad to do so if I can secure the good company of the rest of you, or even some of you."

"Of one in particular, I presume," laughed his brother heartily.

"Will you take us in the yacht, my dear?" asked Violet, addressing her husband.

"If the weather proves suitable we can go in that way—as many as the *Dolphin* can accommodate comfortably. Though probably some of the company would prefer traveling by rail, as the speedier and, at this season, the safer mode," replied Captain Raymond.

"If we take the yacht, you will go with us in it, of course, mamma," observed Violet. "Grandpa and Grandma, too."

"Thank you, daughter, the yacht always seems very pleasant and homelike to me, and I have great confidence in my honored son-in-law as her commander," returned Mrs. Travilla with a smiling look at the captain.

He bowed his acknowledgment, saying, "Thank you, mother, I fully appreciate the kindness of that remark." Then turning to his wife's grandfather, "And you, sir, and your good wife, I hope may feel willing to be of our company should we decide to take the yacht?"

"Thank you, captain. I think it probable we will," Mr. Dinsmore said in reply.

"I hope my three brothers will also be able to accompany us," said Violet.

Neither one of them felt certain of his ability to do so, but all thought it would be a pleasure indeed to visit Florida in such company. No one seemed ready yet for definite arrangements, but as the trip was not to be taken for a month prompt decision was not esteemed necessary. Shortly after tea most of them bade goodnight and left for their homes.

Chester was one of the last to go, but it was not yet very late when Lucilla and Gracie sought their own little sitting room and lingered there for a bit of chat together.

Their father had said they need not hasten with their preparations for bed, as he was coming in presently for a few moments. They had hardly finished their talk when he came in.

"Well, daughters," he said, taking a seat between them on the sofa and putting an arm about the waist of each. "I hope you have enjoyed this first day of a new year?"

"Yes, indeed, papa," both replied. "And we hope you have also," added Gracie.

"I have," he said. "I think we may well be called a happy and favored family. But I wonder," he added with a smiling glance from one to the other, "if my older daughters have not been a trifle disappointed that their father has made them no New Year's gift of any account."

"Why, papa!" they both exclaimed. "You gave us such elegant and costly Christmas gifts and each several valuable books today. We should be very ungrateful if we did not think that quite enough."

"I am well satisfied that you should think it enough," he returned laughingly, "but I do not. Here is something more," as he spoke he took from his pocket two sealed envelopes and put one into the hand of each.

They took them with a pleased, "Oh, thank you very much, papa!" And each hastened to open their own envelope and examine the contents with great eagerness.

"What is it, papa?" asked Gracie with a slightly puzzled look at a folded paper found in hers.

"A certificate of stock which will increase your allowance of pocket money to about ten dollars a week, my dear."

"Oh, how nice! How kind and generous you are, papa!" she exclaimed, putting an arm about his neck and showering kisses on his lips and cheek.

"And mine is just the same, is it not, papa?" asked Lucilla, taking her turn in bestowing upon him the same sort of thanks. "But oh, I am afraid you are giving us more than you can well spare!"

"No, daughter dear," he said. "You need trouble yourselves with no fears on that score. Our kind heavenly Father has so prospered me that I can well afford it. I have confidence in my dear eldest daughters that they will not waste it but will use it wisely and well."

"I hope so, papa," said Gracie. "You have taught us that our money is a talent for which we will have to give an account."

"Yes, daughter, I hope you will always keep that in mind and be neither selfish nor wasteful in the use you put it to."

"I do not mean to be either, papa," she returned. "I may always consult you about it, may I not?"

"Whenever it pleases you to do so I shall be happy to listen and advise you to the best of my ability," he answered with an affectionate look and smile.

CHAPTER THIRD

A FEW DAYS LATER a package of books was received at Woodburn which, upon being opened, proved to be the histories of Florida ordered by the captain from the neighboring city. They were hailed with delight by Violet and the other girls, who were cordially invited to help themselves, study up the subject in private, and report progress in the evenings. Each one of them selected a book, as did the captain also.

"Aren't Elsie and I to help read them, papa?" asked Ned in a slightly disappointed tone.

"You may both do so if you choose," their father replied. "But I hardly think the books will prove juvenile enough to interest you as much as it will to hear from us older ones some account of their contents."

"Oh, yes, papa! And your way is always the best," exclaimed Elsie, her eyes beaming with pleasure. "Neddie," turning to her brother, "you know we always like listening to stories somebody tells us, even better than reading them for ourselves."

"Yes, indeed," he cried. "I like that a great deal better. I guess papa's way is best after all."

Just then Chester came in and, when the usual greetings had been exchanged, "Ah, so they have come—your ordered works on Florida, captain?"

"Yes. Will you help yourself to one or more and join us in the gathering up of information in regard to the history, climate, and productions of that part of the country?"

"Thank you, captain, I will be very glad to do so," was the prompt and pleased reply. "I will be ever so glad to join in your studies now and your visits to the localities afterward."

"That last, I am thinking, will be the pleasantest part," said Gracie. "But it should be all the more enjoyable for doing this part well first."

"Father," said Lucilla, "as you have visited Florida and know a great deal about its history, can't you begin our work of preparation for the trip by telling us something of the facts as we sit in the library after tea tonight?"

"I can if it is desired by all of you," came his pleasant-toned reply.

"Before Neddie and I have to go to bed, papa, please," exclaimed little Elsie coaxingly.

"Yes, daughter, you and Neddie shall be of the audience," replied her father, patting affectionately the little hand she had laid upon his knee. "My lecture will not be a very lengthy one, and if not quite over by your usual bedtime, you and Ned, if not too sleepy to be interested listeners, may stay up until its conclusion."

"Oh, thank you, my dear papa!" exclaimed the little girl joyfully.

"Thank you, papa," said her brother. "I'll not grow sleepy while you are telling the story, unless you make it very dull and stupid."

"Why, son, have I ever done that?" asked his father, looking much amused.

Elsie exclaimed, "Why, Ned! Papa's stories are always ever so nice and interesting."

"They are most always," returned the little fellow, hanging his head and blushing with mortification. "But I have gotten sleepy sometimes because I couldn't help it."

"For which papa doesn't blame his little boy in the least," said the captain soothingly, drawing the little fellow to him and stroking his hair with a caressing hand.

At that moment, wheels were heard on the drive, and Gracie, glancing from the window, exclaimed joyfully, "Oh, here comes the Ion carriage with Grandma Elsie and Evelyn in it. Now, papa, you will have quite an audience."

"If they happen to want the same thing that the rest of you do," returned her father, as he left the room to welcome the visitors and help them alight.

They had come only for a call, but it was not at all difficult to persuade them to stay and spend the night, sending back word to their homes by the coachman. In prospect of their intended visit to Florida, they were both as greatly interested as the others in learning all they could of its history and what would be the best points to visit in search of pleasure and profit.

On leaving the tea table all gathered in the library, the ladies with their fancy needlework, Chester seated near his betrothed, the captain in an easy chair with the little ones close beside him — one at each knee and both looking eagerly expectant. They knew their father to be a good story teller and thought the subject in hand one sure to prove very interesting to them.

After a moment's silence in which the captain seemed to be absorbed in quiet thought, he began.

"In the year 1512—that is nearly four hundred years ago—a Spaniard named Juan Ponce de Leon, who had amassed a fortune by subjugating the natives of the island of Puerto Rico but had grown old and wanted to be young again, had heard of an Indian tradition that there was a land to the north where was a fountain. He was told that bathing in it and drinking of the water freely would restore youth and make one live forever. So, he set sail in search of it, and on the twenty-first day of April, he landed upon the eastern shore of Florida near the mouth of the St. Johns River.

The same day was what Roman Catholics called Paschal Sunday, or the Sunday of the Feast of Flowers, and the land was very beautiful—with magnificent trees of various kinds, stalwart live oaks, tall palm trees, the mournful cypress, and the brilliant dogwood. Waving moss drooped from the hanging boughs of the forest trees; golden fruit and lovely blossoms adorned those of the orange trees; while singing birds filled the air with music, and white-winged water fouls skimmed quietly on the surface of the water. The ground was carpeted with green grass and beautiful flowers of various hues; also in the forest was an abundance of wild game, deer, turkeys, and so forth.

"De Leon thought he had found the paradise of which he was in search. He went up the river, but by mistake he took a chain of lakes, supposing them to be a part of the main river, and finally reached a great sulfur and mineral spring, which is now called by his name. He did not stay long, but soon he sailed southward to the end of the peninsula then back to Puerto Rico. Nine years afterward, he tried to plant a colony in Florida, but the Indians resisted and mortally wounded him. He retreated to Cuba and soon afterward died there."

The captain paused in his narrative, and Elsie asked, "Then did the Spaniards let the Indians have their own country in peace, papa?"

"No," replied her father. "Cortez had meanwhile conquered Mexico, finding quantities of gold there, of which he basely robbed its people. He landed there in 1519 and captured the City of Mexico in 1521.

"In the meantime Narvaez had tried to take possession of Florida and its supposed treasures. He had asked and obtained of the king of Spain authority to conquer and govern it with the title of Adelantado. His dominion would extend from Cape Florida to the River of Palms.

"On the fourteenth of April, he landed near Tampa Bay with four hundred armed men and eighty horses.

"He and his men were entirely unsuccessful. They found no gold; the Indians were hostile; provisions scarce; and finally they built boats in which to escape from Florida. The boats were of a very rude sort, and the men knew nothing about managing them. So, though they set sail, it was to make a most unsuccessful voyage. They nearly perished with cold and hunger, and many were drowned in the sea. The boat that carried Narvaez was driven out to sea and nothing more was ever heard of him. Not more than four of his followers escaped."

The captain paused for a moment. Then, turning to his wife, he said pleasantly, "Well, my dear, suppose you take your turn now as narrator and give us a brief sketch of the doings of Fernando de Sota, the Spaniard who next undertook to conquer Florida."

"Yes," said Violet, "I have been reading his story today with great interest, and though I cannot hope to nearly equal my husband as narrator, I shall just do the best I can.

"History tells us that Cabeca de Vaca—one of the four survivors of the ill-fated expedition of Narvaez—went back to Spain. For purposes of his own, he spread abroad the story that Florida was the richest country yet discovered. That raised a great furor for going there. De Sota began preparations for an expedition, and nobles and gentlemen contended for the privilege of joining it.

"On the eighteenth day of May in 1539, de Sota left Cuba with one thousand men-at-arms and 350 horses. He landed at Tampa Bay—on the west coast—on Whitsunday, the twenty-fifth of May. His force was larger and of more respectable quality than any that had preceded it. And he was not so bad and cruel a man as his predecessor—Narvaez."

"Did Narvaez do very bad things to the poor Indians, mamma?" asked Elsie.

"Yes, indeed, Elsie!" replied her mother. "In his treatment of them, he showed himself a most cruel, heartless wretch. Wilmer, in his 'Ferdinand de Sota,' tells of a chief whom he calls Cacique Ucita, who, after forming a treaty of peace and amity with Pamphilo de Narvaez, had been most outrageously abused by him. His aged mother was torn to pieces by dogs in his absence from home, and when he returned and showed his grief and anger, he himself was seized, and his nose was cut off."

"Oh, mamma, how very, very cruel!" cried Elsie. "Had Ucita's mother done anything to Narvaez to make him treat her so?"

"Nothing except that she complained to her son of a Spaniard who had treated a young Indian girl very badly.

"Narvaez had shown himself an atrociously cruel man. So, it was no wonder the poor Indians hated him. How could anything else be expected of poor Ucita, when he learned of the dreadful, undeserved death his poor mother had to die, than that he would be, as he was, frantic with grief and anger and make, as he did, threats of terrible vengeance against the Spaniards? But instead of acknowledging his cruelty and trying to make some amends, as I have said, Narvaez ordered him to be seized, scourged, and sadly mutilated.

"Then, as soon as Ucita's subjects heard of all this, they hastened from every part of his dominion to avenge him upon the Spaniards. Perceiving their danger, the Spaniards then fled with all expedition, and so they barely escaped the vengeance they so richly deserved.

"But to go back to my story of de Soto—he had landed a few miles from an Indian town that stood on the site of the present town of Tampa. He had with him two Indians whom he had been training for guides and interpreters. But to his great disappointment, they escaped.

"The Spaniards had captured some Indian women, and from them De Soto learned that a neighboring chief had in his keeping a captured Spaniard, one of the men of Narvaez.

"After Narvaez landed, he had sent back to Cuba one of his smaller vessels—on board of which was this Juan Ortiz—to carry the news of his safe arrival to his wife. She at once sent additional supplies by the same vessel, and it reached the bay the day after

Narvaez and his men fled, as I have already told you, from the vengeance of the outraged Ucita and his indignant subjects.

"Ortiz and those with him, seeing a letter fixed in a cleft of a stick on shore, asked some of the Indians whom they saw to bring it to them. They refused and made signs for the Spaniards to come for it. Juan Ortiz, then a boy of eighteen, with some comrades took a boat and went on shore, when they were at once seized by the Indians. One of them, who resisted, was instantly killed, and the rest were taken to the cruelly wronged and enraged chief Ucita, who had made a vow to punish with death any Spaniard who should fall into his hands.

"Ortiz's mind, as they hurried him onward, was filled with the most horrible forebodings. When they reached the village, the chief was waiting in the public square to receive them. One of the Spaniards was at once seized, stripped of his clothes, and bade run for his life.

The square was enclosed by palisades, and the only gateway was guarded by well-armed Indians. As soon as the naked Spaniard began to run, one of the Indians shot an arrow, the barbed edge of which sank deeply into his shoulder. Another and another arrow followed, the man in a frenzy of pain hurrying round and round in a desperate effort to find some opening by which he might escape, the Indians looking on with evident delight.

"This scene lasted more than an hour, and when the wretched victim fell to the ground, there were no less than thirty arrows fixed in his flesh. The whole surface of his body was covered with blood.

"The Indians let him lie there in a dying condition and chose another victim to go through the same tortures—then another and another till all were slain except Ortiz. By that time, the Indians seemed to be tired of the cruel sport, and he saw them consulting together, the chief apparently giving the others some directions.

"It would seem that from some real or fancied resemblance Ucita saw in the lad to the cruel wretch, Pamphilo de Narvaez, he supposed him to be a relative. Therefore, he intended him to suffer some even more agonizing death than that just meted out to his fellows. For that purpose, some of them now busied themselves in making a wooden frame. They laid parallel to each other two stout pieces of wood—six or seven feet long and three feet apart—and laid a number of others across them so as to form a sort of grate or hurdle to which they then bound Ortiz with leather thongs. They then placed it on four stakes driven into the ground and kindled a fire underneath, using for it such things as would burn slowly, scarcely making a blaze."

"Oh, mamma! Were they going to burn him to death?" exclaimed Elsie, aghast with horror.

"Sadly, yes," replied her mother. "He was soon suffering terribly. One of the Indian women who was present felt sorry for him and hastened away to the house of Ucita and told his daughter Ulelah what was going on. She was a girl of eighteen and not so hard as the men. She was sorry for the poor young man and made haste to run to the scene of his sufferings, where he was shrieking with pain and begging for mercy.

"Hearing these sounds before she reached the spot, she ran faster and got there panting for breath. At once, she threw herself at her father's feet and begged him to stop the execution for a few minutes.

He did so, ordering some of the men to lift the frame to which Ortiz was fastened and lay it on the ground. Ulelah then begged her father to remember that Ortiz had never offended him, and that it would be more humane — more to his honor — to keep him as a prisoner than to put him to death without any reason or justification.

"The chief sternly replied that he had sentenced the Spaniard to death and no consideration should prevent him from executing him. Then Ulelah begged him to put it off for a day that was annually celebrated as a religious festival, at which time he might be offered as a sacrifice to their gods.

"To that at length Ucita consented. Ortiz was unbound, and the princess placed him under the care of the best physician of their tribe.

"As soon as Ortiz began to recover, every care was taken that he should not escape. He was made to busy himself in the most laborious and slavish occupations. Sometimes he was compelled to run incessantly, from the raising of the sun to its setting, in the public square where his comrades had been put to death. Indians armed with bows and arrows stood ready to shoot him if he should halt for a moment. That over, he would lie exhausted and almost insensible on the hard earthen floor of a hut, the best lodging the chief would allow him.

"At such time, Ulelah and her maids would come to him with food, restoratives, medicines, and words of consolation and encouragement — all of which helped him to live and endure.

"When Ortiz had been there about nine months, the Princess Ulelah came to him one evening and told him that their religious festival should be celebrated on the first day of the new moon. Ortiz had heard that the chief intended to sacrifice him on that occasion, and, of course, he was sorely distressed at the dreadful prospect before him. As the time drew near, he tried to prepare his mind for his doom, for he could see no way of escape. Ulelah told him she had done all she could to induce her father to spare his life, but she could gain nothing more than a promise to delay the execution of the sentence for a year—on one condition. He had to keep guard over the cemetery of the tribe, where, according to the custom of their people, the bodies of the dead were exposed above the ground until the flesh wasted away, leaving only the naked skeletons.

"The cemetery was about three miles from the village in an open space of ground surrounded by forests. The bodies lay on biers on stages raised several feet above the ground, and it was necessary to keep a watch over them every night to protect them from the wild beasts of prey in the surrounding woods. Generally those who were compelled to keep watch were criminals under sentence of death, who were permitted to live, if they could, so long as they performed that duty faithfully. But they ran great risks from the wild beasts of prey in the surrounding forests and from effluvia arising from the decaying bodies.

"It seemed a terrible alternative, but Ortiz took it rather than suffer immediate death. Ulelah wept over him, and her sympathy abated something of the horror of his hard fate and helped him to meet it manfully.

"The next day, he was taken to the place by the chief's officers, who gave him a bow and arrows and other weapons, told him to be vigilant, and warned him against any attempt to escape.

"His little hut of reeds was in the midst of the cemetery. The stench was horrible, and for several hours, it overpowered him with sickness and stupor such as he had never known before. From that, he partially recovered before night, and toward morning the howling of wolves helped to arouse him. Presently, he nearly lost consciousness again.

"In the early part of the night, he had contrived to scare away the wolves by waving the lighted torch, which was kept ready for the purpose. At length, he became conscious that some living thing was near him, as he could hear the sound of breathing. By the light of his torch, he saw a very large animal dragging away the body of a child.

"Before he could arouse himself sufficiently to attack the animal, it had reached the woods and was out of sight. He was very ill, but he roused all his energies, fitted an arrow to his bow and staggered toward that part of the forest where the beast had disappeared. As he reached the edge of the wood, he heard a sound like the gnawing of a bone. He could not see the creature that made it, but he sent an arrow in the direction of the sound, and at the same moment, he fell to the ground in a faint. That exertion had entirely exhausted his small portion of strength.

"There he lay till daybreak. Recovering slight consciousness, he by great and determined effort managed to crawl back to his hut.

"Some time later came the officers whose duty it was to make a daily examination. They at once missed the child's body and were about to dash out the brains of Ortiz, but he made haste to tell of his night adventure. They went to the part of the forest that he pointed out as the spot where he had fired at the wild animal, found the body of the child, and lying near it, that of a large, dead animal of the tiger kind. The arrow of Ortiz had struck it between the shoulders, penetrated to the heart, and doubtless killed it instantly.

"The Indians greatly admired the skill Ortiz had shown by that shot, and as they recovered the body of the child they held him blameless.

"Gradually he grew accustomed to that tainted air and strong enough to drive away wolves, killing several of them. The Indian officers brought him provisions, and so he lived for about two weeks. Then one night, he was alarmed by the sound of footsteps that sounded like those of human beings. He thought some new trouble was coming upon him, but as they drew near, he saw by the light of his torch that they were three women—the Princess Ulelah and two female attendants. He recognized the princess by her graceful form and the richness of her dress. She told him the priests of her tribe would not consent to any change of his sentence or delay in carrying it out. Ucita had promised them he should be sacrificed at the approaching festival, and they were determined not to allow their deity to be defrauded of his victim. She said she had exposed herself to great risk by coming to warn him of his danger, for if the priests should learn that she had helped him escape they would take her life—not even her father's authority could save her from them. To save his life, she advised him to fly at once.

"He thought all this proved that she loved him and told her he loved her. He told her that in his own country, he belonged to an ancient and honorable family and was heir to a large estate. He begged her to go with him and become his wife.

"When he had finished speaking, she was silent for a few moments. She then answered in a tone that seemed to show some displeasure. 'I regret,' she said, 'that any part of my conduct should have led you into so great an error. In all my efforts to serve you I have had no motive but those of humanity. I would have done no less for any other human being in the same circumstance. To fully convince you of your mistake, I will tell you that I am betrothed to a neighboring cacique, to whose protection I am about to recommend you. Before daybreak, I will send a faithful guide to conduct you to the village. Lose no time on the way, and when you are presented to Mocoso, give him this girdle as a token that you come from me. He will then consider himself honor bound to defend you from all danger at the hazard of his own life.'

"Ulelah and her maidens then left him. Before morning came the promised guide, who conducted Ortiz through the trackless forest in a northerly direction, urging him to walk very fast, as he would certainly be pursued as soon as his absence was discovered.

"In telling his story afterward, Ortiz said they traveled about eight leagues and reached Mocoso's village, at whose entrance the guide, fearing to be recognized by some one of Mocoso's subjects, left him to enter it alone.

"Some Indians were fishing in a stream near by. They saw Ortiz come out of the woods, and frightened by his outlandish appearance, they snatched up their arms with the intention of attacking him. When he showed the girdle that Ulelah had given him, they understood that he was the bearer of a message to their chief. One of them came forward to give the usual welcome, and then they led him to the village, where his Spanish dress, which he still wore, attracted much attention. He was ushered into the presence of Mocoso and found that chief a youthful Indian of noble bearing, tall and graceful in person and possessed of a handsome and intelligent face. Ortiz presented the girdle. Mocoso examined it attentively and greatly to the surprise of Ortiz seemed to gain from it as much information as if its ornamental work had been in written words.

"Presently raising his eyes from the girdle Mocoso said, 'Christian, I am requested to protect you, and it shall be done. You are safe in my village, but do not venture beyond it, or you may have the misfortune to be recaptured by your enemies.'

"From that time Mocoso treated Ortiz with the affection of a brother."

"Oh, how nice!" exclaimed little Elsie. "But when Ucita heard that Ortiz was gone, what did he do about it?"

"When he heard where he was hiding, he sent ambassadors to demand that he be given up. Mocoso refused. That caused a misunderstanding between the two chiefs and delayed the marriage of Ulelah and Mocoso for several years. At the end of three years, the priests interposed, and the wedding was allowed to take place. But the two chiefs did not become reconciled and held no communication with each other.

"For twelve years, Ortiz was kept in safety by Mocoso. Then de Soto and his men came, and Ortiz, hearing of their arrival, wanted to join them. He set out to do so in the company of some of his Indian friends.

"At the same time, a Spaniard named Porcella had started out to hunt some Indians for slaves. On his way, he saw Ortiz with his party of ten or twelve Indians, and with uplifted weapons, he and his men spurred their horses toward them. All but one fled. This one, Ortiz, drew near and, speaking in Spanish, said, 'Cavaliers, do not kill me. I am one of your own countrymen. I beg that you not molest these Indians who are with me; for I am indebted to them for the preservation of my life.'

"He then made signs for his Indian friends to come back, which some few did, and he and they were taken on horseback behind some of the cavaliers and so conveyed to de Soto's camp where Ortiz told his story — the very same that I have been telling you.

"'As soon as Mocoso heard of your arrival,' he went on, 'he asked me to come to you with the offer of his friendship, and I was on my way to your camp with several of his officers when I met your cavaliers.'

"While listening to this long story, de Soto's sympathies had been much excited for Ortiz. He at once presented him with a fine horse, a suit of handsome clothes, and all the arms and equipments of a captain of the cavalry.

"Then he sent two Indians back to Mocoso with a message, accepting his offers of friendship and inviting him to visit the camp. Mocoso did so shortly afterward, bringing with him some of his principal warriors. His appearance and fine manners were such as at once to prepossess the Spaniards in his favor. De Soto received him with cordiality and thanked him for his kindness to the Spaniard who had sought his protection.

"Mocoso's reply was one that could not fail to be pleasing to the Spaniards. It was that he had done nothing deserving of thanks; that Ortiz had come to him well recommended; and that his honor was pledged for his safety. 'His own valor and other good qualities,' he added, 'entitled him to all the respect which I and my people could show him. My acquaintance with him disposes me to be friendly to all his countrymen.'

"The historian goes on to tell us that when Mocoso's mother heard where he had gone, she was terrified at the thought of what injury might be done to him—no doubt remembering the sad misfortune of Ucita and his mother so cruelly dealt with by the treacherous Spaniards. In the greatest distress, she hurried to the camp of de Soto and implored him to set her son at liberty and not treat him as Ucita had been treated by Narvaez. 'If he has offended you,' she said, 'consider that he is but young and look upon his fault as one of the common indiscretions of youth. Let him go back to his people, and I will remain here and undergo whatever sufferings you may choose to inflict.'"

"What a good, kind mother!" exclaimed little Elsie. "I certainly hope they didn't hurt her or her son, either."

"No," said her mother. "De Soto tried hard to convince her that he considered himself under obligation to Mocoso and that he had only intended to treat him in a most friendly manner. But all he could say did not remove the anxiety of the poor, frightened woman, for she had come to believe the whole Spanish nation treacherous and cruel. Mocoso himself at last persuaded her that he was entirely free to go or stay as he pleased. Still, she could not altogether banish her fears, and before leaving, she took Juan Ortiz aside and entreated him to watch over the safety of his friend and especially to take heed that the other Spaniards did not poison him."

"Did Mocoso stay long? And did they harm him, mamma?" asked Elsie.

"He stayed eight days in the Spanish camp," replied Violet, "being inspired with perfect confidence in the Christians."

"Christians, mamma? What Christians?" asked Ned curiously.

"That was what the Spaniards called themselves," she answered. "But it was a sad misnomer. For theirs seemed to be anything else than the spirit of Christ, my son."

CHAPTER FOURTH

THE NEXT EVENING the same company, with some additions, gathered in the library at Woodburn, all full of interest in the history of Florida and anxious to learn what they could of its climate, productions, and anything that might be known of the tribes of Indians inhabiting it before the invasion of the Spaniards.

At the earnest request of the others, Grandma Elsie was the first narrator of the evening.

"I have been reading Wilmer's *Travels and Adventures of de Soto*" she said. "He tells much that is interesting in regard to the Indians inhabiting Florida when the Spaniards invaded it. One tribe was the Natchez, and he says that they and other tribes made some progress in civilization. But the effect of that invasion was a relapse into barbarism from which they have never recovered. At the time of de Soto's coming, they had none of the nomadic habits for which the North American Indians have since been remarkable. They then lived in permanent habitations and cultivated the land, deriving their subsistence chiefly from it, though practicing hunting and fishing, partly for subsistence and partly for sport. They were not entirely ignorant of some arts and manufacturing, and some which they practiced were extremely ingenious. They had domestic utensils and household furniture that were both artistic and elegant. Their dresses, especially those of the females, were very tasteful and ornate. Some specimens of their earthenware are still preserved and are highly creditable to their skill in that branch of industry. Among their household goods, they had boxes made of split cane and other materials, ingeniously wrought and ornamented and also mats for their floors. Their apparel was composed partly of skins handsomely dressed and colored and partly of a sort of woven cloth made of the fibrous bark of the mulberry tree and a certain species of wild hemp. Their finest fabrics, used by the wives and daughters of the caciques, were obtained from the bark of the young mulberry shoots beaten into small fibers, then bleached, and twisted or spun into threads of a convenient size for weaving. This was done in a very simple manner by driving small stakes into the ground, stretching a warp across from one to another, then inserting the weft by using the fingers instead of a shuttle. By this tedious process, they made very beautiful shawls and mantillas with fringed borders of most exquisite patterns."

"They must have been very industrious, I think," said little Elsie.

"Yes," assented her grandmother. "The weavers I presume were women, but the men also seemed to have been industrious. They manufactured articles of gold, silver, and copper. None of iron, however. Some of their axes, hatchets, and weapons of war were made of copper, and they, like the Peruvians, possessed the art of imparting a temper to that metal which made it nearly equal to iron for the manufacture of edged tools. The Peruvians, it is said, used an alloy of copper and tin for much the same purpose. It is supposed that this alloy may perhaps be even harder than brass, which is composed chiefly of copper and zinc."

"Had they good houses to live in, grandma?" asked Ned.

"Yes," she replied. "Even those of the common people were much better than the log huts of our Western settlers or the turf-built shanties of the Irish peasantry. Some were thirty feet square and contained several rooms each, and some had cellars in which the people stored their grain. The houses of the caciques were built on mounds or terraces, and sometimes they had porticos. The walls were hung with prepared buckskins that resembled tapestries, while others had carpets of the same material. Some of their temples had sculptured ornaments. A Portuguese gentleman tells of one on the roof or cupola of a temple that was a carved bird with gilded eyes.

"The religion of the Natchez resembled that of the Peruvians. They worshipped the sun as the source of light and heat or a symbol of the divine goodness and wisdom. They believed in the immortality of the human soul and in future rewards and punishments, in the existence of a supreme and omnipotent Deity called the Great Spirit, and also in an evil spirit of inferior power, who was supposed to govern the seasons and control the elements. They seem not to have been image-worshippers until the Spaniards made them such. Their government was somewhat despotic, but not tyrannical. They were ruled by their chiefs, whose authority was patriarchal."

Grandma Elsie paused as if she had finished her narration, and Ned exclaimed, "Oh, that isn't all, grandma, is it?"

"All of my part of the account, for the present at least," she said with her sweet smile. Then turning to Lucilla, "You will tell us the story of the Princess Xualla, will you not?"

"You could surely do it much better than I, Grandma Elsie," was the modest rejoinder. "But if you wish it, I will do my best."

"We do," replied several voices, and Lucilla, encouraged by a look and smile from her father that seemed to speak confidence in her story-telling abilities, at once began.

"It seems that de Soto, not finding there the gold for which he had come and encouraged by the Indians, who wanted to be rid of him, to think that it might be discovered in regions still remote, started again upon his quest, taking a northerly or northwesterly direction.

"As they journeyed on they came to a part of Florida governed by a female cacique—a beautiful young girl called the Princess Xualla. Her country was a fine, open one and well cultivated. They reached the neighborhood of her capital—a town on the farther side of a river—about an hour before nightfall. Here they encamped and were about to seize some Indians to get from them information of the country and people. But some others on the farther side of the stream hastened over in a canoe to ask what was wanted.

"De Soto had had a chair of state placed on the margin of the stream and placed himself in it. The Indians saluted him and asked whether he was for peace or war. He responded that he wished to be at peace and hoped they would supply him with provisions for his army.

"They answered that they wished to be at peace, but the season had been one of scarcity and they barely had enough food for themselves. Their land, they said, was governed by a maiden lady, and they would report to her of the arrival of the strangers and what they demanded.

"They then returned to their canoe and paddled back to the town to carry the news to the princess and chieftans. The Spaniards, watching the canoe, saw those in it received by a crowd of their countrymen at the landing place and that their news seemed to cause some commotion. But soon several canoes left the wharf and came toward the Spaniards. The first was fitted with a tasteful canopy and various decorations. It was filled with women all brightly dressed, among them the princess, the splendor of whose appearance almost dazzled the eyes of the beholder. There were five or six other canoes, which held her principal officers and attendants.

"When the boats reached the shore, the Indians disembarked and placed a seat for their lady opposite to de Soto's chair of state. She saluted the strangers with grace and dignity. Then, taking her seat, she waited in silence as if expecting her visitors to begin the conference.

"For several minutes, de Soto gazed upon her with feelings of admiration and reverence. He had seldom seen a more beautiful female or one in whom conscious pride of elevated rank was so nicely balanced with womanly reserve and youthful modesty. She seemed about nineteen years of age. She had perfectly regular features, an intellectual countenance, and a beautiful form. She was richly dressed, her robe and mantilla of the finest woven cloth of native manufacture and as white and as delicate of texture as the finest linen of Europe. Her garments were bordered with a rich brocade composed of feathers and beads of various colors interwoven with the material of the cloth. She wore also a profusion of pearls and some glittering ornaments that the Spaniards supposed to be made of gold. Her name was Xualla, and she ruled over several provinces.

"Juan Ortiz, being acquainted with several Indian dialects, acted as interpreter and told of the needs of the Spaniards. Xualla was sorry the harvest had been so poor that she had little ability to relieve their wants. She invited them to fix their quarters in her principal village while it was convenient for them to stay in the neighborhood. Then she took from her neck a necklace of pearls of great value and requested Juan Ortiz to present it to the governor, as it would not be modest for her to give it herself.

"De Soto arose, took it respectfully, and presented a ruby ring in return, taking it from his own finger. That seems to have been a ratification of peace between them. The Spanish troops were taken over the river and quartered in the public square in the center of town, and the princess sent them a supply of good provisions and poultry and other delicacies for de Soto's table.

"Xualla's mother was living in retirement about twelve leagues from her daughter's capital. Xualla invited her to come and see these strange people — the Spaniards — but she declined and reproved her daughter for entertaining travelers of whom she knew nothing. Events soon showed that she was right. Sadly, the Spaniards, acting with their usual perfidy, made Xualla a prisoner, robbed the people, the temples, and burial places, and tried to get possession of her mother. Xualla was urged and probably finally compelled by threats to direct them to her mother's abode.

"A young warrior, evidently occupying some prominent position under her government, was given directions that were not heard or understood by the Spaniards. He made a sign of obedience then turned to the Spaniards and made them understand that he was ready to be their conductor. One of them, named Juan Anasco, had been selected to go in search of the widow, and now thirty Spaniards, under his command, started on that errand.

"As they proceeded on their way, the young chief seemed to grow more melancholy. After traveling about five miles, they stopped for a rest, and while the soldiers were taking some refreshments, the guide sat in pensive silence by the side of the road, refusing to partake of the repast. He laid aside his mantle, or cloak, which was made of the finest of sable furs, took off his quiver, and began to draw out the arrows one by one.

"The curiosity of the Spaniards was excited. They drew near and admired the arrows, which were made of reeds, feathered with the dark plumage of a crow or raven. They were variously pointed, some with bones properly shaped, others with barbs of very hard wood, while the last one in the quiver was armed with a piece of flint cut in a triangular form and was exceedingly sharp. This he held in his hand while the Spaniards were examining the others, and suddenly he plunged the barb of flint into his throat and fell dead.

"The other Indians stood aghast and began to fill the air with their lamentations. From them, I presume, the Spaniards then learned that the young chief was affianced to the princess and was very much beloved and respected by the whole nation. He had committed suicide to escape betraying the mother of his betrothed into the hands of the Spaniards. In obedience to the order of the princess, he had undertaken to guide those cruel enemies to the widow's hiding place, but he well knew that she was forced to give the order and that the carrying out of it would be the cause of increased trouble to her and her parent. He had told one of the Indians who were of the party that it would be better for him to die than to be the means of increasing the afflictions of those whom he so dearly loved.

"The grief and despair of Xualla, when she heard of the death of her betrothed, were so great that even the Spaniards were moved to pity. For several days, she shut herself up in her own dwelling and was not seen by either the Spaniards or her own people.

"In the meantime, the Spaniards were robbing the tombs and temples of the country, finding great spoil there.

"About a week after the death of the young chief, de Soto told Xualla she must send another guide with a party of Spaniards to her mother's habitation. She promptly and decidedly refused to do so, saying she had been justly punished once for consenting to place her poor mother in his power. She went on to say that no fears for herself would ever make her do so again. She said he had made her as miserable as she could be, and now she defied him. She wished she had listened to the advice of her wise counselors and driven him away from her shores when he first came with his false and deceitful promises of peace and friendship. She would have saved herself from that sorrow and remorse, which now made her life insupportable. 'Why do you remain in my country?' she asked. 'Are there no other lands to be robbed, no other people to be made miserable? Here there is nothing for you to do. You have taken all we had, and you can add nothing to our wretchedness. Go, coward as you are! Cease to make war on helpless women, and if you must be a villain, let your conduct prove that you are a man!'"

"I think she was very brave to talk to him in that way," said Elsie. "Did he kill her for it?"

"No," replied Lucilla. "Actually, he was polite and courteous as usual, but he told her that the King of Spain was the true sovereign and lawful proprietor of the country over which she claimed to be princess. He also told her that, in all those matters which had offended her, the Spanish army had acted under the authority of that great monarch—the monarch to whom she herself was bound to render obedience.

"Next he told her that she must accompany the Spaniards on their march as far as the border of her dominions and that she would be expected to control her subjects and to make them entirely submissive to the Spaniards. He promised that she should be treated with the respect and dignity due her rank and sex.

"But the one who tells the story says she did not receive the respect she deserved. It was on the third day of May in 1540, that the Spaniards left Cofachiqui, compelling the princess to accompany them and requiring her to call upon her subjects to carry burdens for them from one stopping place to another. They passed through a delightful valley called Xualla, which had many groves, plantations, and pasture grounds. On the seventh day, they came to a province called Chulaque, supposed to have been inhabited by a tribe of Cherokee. But before the Spaniards had reached this point, Xualla had contrived to escape, assisted by two of her female slaves who were in attendance upon her."

"Oh, I hope they didn't catch her again—the Spaniards, I mean," exclaimed Ned.

"No," replied Lucilla. "De Soto would not allow her to be pursued."

"Did he and his men stay there in that beautiful valley, Lu?" asked Elsie.

"No, as he could not find the gold he so coveted in Florida, he traveled on in a westerly direction till he reached the Mississippi—a hard journey through wilderness of forests and marshes. He could nowhere find the gold he so coveted, became discouraged and worn out, was stricken with malignant fever, and died on the banks of the Mississippi in June of 1542."

"A victim to the love of gold, like so many of his countrymen," sighed Grandma Elsie. "The Bible tells us 'the love of money is the root of all evil,' and history repeats the lesson. The love of money led to Pizarro's wicked attack upon the Peruvians, and the conquest of that country was a source of trouble and calamity to all, or nearly all who were concerned with it. As soon as de Soto left, after the capture of Cuzco, the victors began to quarrel with each other for the spoils. Almagro provoked a war with Pizarro, was taken prisoner, and strangled.

Gonzalo Pizarro was beheaded by his own countrymen. Another of the brothers, Hernando, returned to Spain, where he was thrown into prison and kept there for many years. Francisco Pizarro himself fell victim to the resentment of Almagro's soldiers. He was assaulted in his own palace, where he had just finished his dinner when the avengers entered. All his servants and guests except his half-brother, Martinez de Alcantara, instantly fled and abandoned him to his fate. It was midday when the assassins entered the palace with drawn weapons and loudly proclaiming their intention to kill the tyrant. There were upward of a thousand persons in the plaza, but no one opposed them. They merely looked coldly on, saying to each other, 'These men are going to kill the governor.'"

"He deserved it for killing Almagro, didn't he, grandma?" asked Ned.

"He certainly did," replied Grandma Elsie. "But they should, if possible, have given him a trial at least. Everyone has a right to that. It is right that murderers should be put to death, but lawfully. The Bible says, 'Whoso sheddeth man's blood, by man shall his blood be shed.' History tells us it is probable that not more than twenty Spaniards in getting mastery of the great empire of Peru—one of the largest upon earth—became rich. In the end, they made nothing, and all that they had gained was ruin—individual and national. Few, if any of them, carried back to their own land any evidences of their success. They dissipated their ill-gotten riches in riotous living or lost them by unfortunate speculations.

"I must tell you of the fate of another of Pizarro's band—the priest Vincent, or Valverde. Vincent counseled, or consented to, many of the enormous crimes committed by that monster of cruelty and avarice, Pizarro, who, after some years of their association in crime, made him Bishop of Cuzco. In November of 1541, Vincent went with a considerable number of Spaniards who had served under Pizarro to the island of Puna, where they were all massacred by the Indians. On that very island, about nine years before, Pizarro had butchered the people, Vincent conniving the crime. The historian says: 'The murderers slandered the Archangel Michael by pretending that he assisted them in their bloody performance; but no angel interposed when Vincent and his fellow assassins were about to be put to death by the infidels.'"

CHAPTER FIFTH

THE NEXT DAY, by Grandma Elsie's invitation, the students of the history of Florida gathered at Ion, and Chester took his turn in relating some of the facts he had come upon in his reading.

"De Soto," he said, "died in June of 1542. Nearly twenty years later—in February of 1562—two good vessels under the command of Jean Ribaut, a French naval officer of experience and repute, were sent out by Admiral Coligny. He was the chief of the Protestants in France, and his desire was to establish colonies in unexplored countries where the Protestants would be at liberty to follow the dictates of their consciences without fear of persecution.

"The admiral obtained a patent from Charles IX, armed those two ships, put in them 550 veteran soldiers and sailors and many young noblemen who embarked as volunteers, and appointed Ribaut as commander.

"They made a prosperous voyage, going directly to the coast of Florida and avoiding the routes in which they were likely to meet Spanish vessels, as the success of their expedition depended upon secrecy.

"On the thirtieth of April, they sighted a cape which Ribaut named Francois. It is now one of the headlands of Matanzas inlet. The next day he discovered the mouth of a river that he named May, because they entered it on the first day of that month. Now it is called the St. Johns. Here they landed and erected a monument of stone with the arms of France engraved upon it. It is said to have been placed upon a little sand hillock in the river. They re-embarked and sailed northward, landing occasionally and finding themselves well received by the many Indians, to whom they made little presents such as looking glasses and bracelets. They continued to sail northward till they entered the harbor of Port Royal, where they anchored. There they built a small fort upon a little island and called it Fort Charles in honor of the King of France.

"Ribaut then selected twenty-five men to remain in the fort, and one of his trusted lieutenants, Charles d'Albert, to command them. He gave them a supply of ammunition and provisions and left them with a parting salute of artillery, replied to from the fort. With that, the vessels sailed away for France, from which they had been absent about four months.

"For some time the colony prospered and made various excursions among the Indians, who received and treated them well. But finally this effort to found a colony proved a failure.

"In 1564, Rene de Laudonniere was charged with the direction of a new one—this also sent out by Coligny. Three vessels were given him, and Charles IX made him a present of fifty thousand crowns. He took with him skillful workmen and several young gentlemen who had asked permission to go at their own expense. He landed in Florida on the twenty-second of June, sailed up the River St. Johns, and began the building of a fort that he named Caroline in honor of the king.

"The Indians proved friendly, but soon the young gentlemen who had volunteered to come with him complained of being forced to labor like common workmen. Fearing that they would excite a mutiny, he sent the most turbulent of them back to France on one of his vessels.

"But the trouble increased among the remaining colonists, and he sent part of them out under the orders of his lieutenant to explore the country. A few days later some sailors fled, taking with them the two boats used in procuring provisions. Others, who had left France only with the hope of making their fortunes, seized one of his ships and went cruising in the Gulf of Mexico. The deserters had also had a bad influence upon the Indians, who now refused to supply the colonists with provisions, and they were soon threatened with famine. I cannot see why they should have been with an abundance of fish in the river and sea and wild game and fruits in the woods," remarked Chester, but then went on with his story. "The historians tell us that they lived for some time on acorns and roots and, when at the last extremity, were saved by the arrival of Captain John Hawkins on August 3, 1565. He showed them great kindness, furnishing them with provisions and selling Laudonniere one of his ships in which they might return to France.

"In telling the story of his visit to Florida, Hawkins mentions the abundance of tobacco, sorrel, maize, and grapes and ascribes the failure of the French colony 'to their lack of thrift, as in such a climate and soil, with marvelous store of deer and diverse other beasts, all men may live.'

"After landing his troops, Ribault went to explore the country, leaving some of his men to guard the ships. Ribault's arrival was on the twenty-ninth of August. On the fourth of September, the French in his vessels sighted a large fleet approaching and asked their object. 'I am Pedro Menendez de Aviles, who has come to hang and behead all Protestants in these regions,' was the haughty reply of the fleet's commander. 'If I find any Catholic, he shall be well treated, but every heretic shall die.'

"The French fleet, surprised and not strong enough to cope with the Spaniards, cut their cables and left. Menendez entered an inlet, which he called St. Augustine, and there began to entrench himself.

"Ribault called together all his forces and resolved to attack the Spaniards contrary to the advice of Laudonniere and all his officers. On the tenth of September, he embarked for that purpose, but he was scarcely at sea when a hurricane dispersed his fleet. Then the Spaniards attacked Fort Caroline.

"Laudonniere was still in the fort, but he was sick and had only about a hundred men, scarcely twenty of them capable of bearing arms. The Spaniards took the fort, massacred the sick, the women and children, and hanged the soldiers who fell into their hands.

"After doing all he could to defend the fort, Laudonniere cut his way through the enemy and plunged into the woods, where he found some of his soldiers who had escaped. He said what he could for encouragement, and during the night he led them to the seashore, where they found a son of Ribaut with three vessels. On one of these—a small brig—Laudonniere, Jacques Ribaut, and a few others escaped from the Spaniards and carried the news of the disaster to France.

"Laudonniere's purpose had been to rejoin and help Jean Ribaut, but his vessel being driven out to sea, he was unable to carry out that intention.

"Three days after the fort was taken, Ribaut's ships were wrecked near Cape Canaveral, and he at once marched in three divisions toward Fort Caroline. When the first division came near the site of the fort, they were attacked by Spaniards, surrendered to Menendez, and were all put to death. A few days later Ribaut arrived with his party, and as Menendez pledged his word that they should be spared, they surrendered. But all were murdered, Menendez killing Ribaut with his own hands. Their bodies were hung on the surrounding trees with the inscription, 'Executed, not as Frenchmen, but as Lutherans.'"

"Lutherans?" echoed Ned inquiringly.

"Yes, meaning Protestants," replied Chester. "That was an age of great cruelty. Satan was very busy, and multitudes were called upon to seal their testimony to Christ with their blood.

"But to go on with the story. About two years after, a gallant Frenchman—Dominic de Gourgues, by name—got up an expedition to avenge the massacre of his countrymen by the Spaniards at Fort Caroline. He came to Florida with three small vessels and 184 men, secured the help of the natives, attacked the fort—now called by the Spaniards Fort San Mateo—and captured the entire garrison. Many of the captives were killed by the Indians, and the rest De Gourgues hanged upon the tree on which Menendez had hanged the Huguenots, putting over the corpses the inscription, "I do this, not as to Spaniards, nor as to outcasts, but as to traitors, theives, and murderers.' His work of revenge accomplished, De Gourgues set sail for France."

"Oh," sighed little Elsie, "what dreadful things people did do in those days! I'm glad I didn't live then instead of now."

"As we all are," responded her mother, "glad for you and for ourselves."

"Yes," said Chester. "I think I have now come to a suitable stopping place. There seems to me little more in Florida's history that we need recount."

"No," said Grandma Elsie, "it seems to me to be nothing but a round of building and destroying, fighting and bloodshed, kept up between the Spaniards and the French with the English also taking part now and again. In 1762, the British captured Havana, and in the treaty following the next year, Great Britain gave Cuba to Spain in exchange for Florida.

"Florida took no part in the Revolutionary War and became a refuge for many loyalists, as it was afterward for fugitive slaves. In 1783, Florida was returned to Spanish rule, Great Britain exchanging it for the Bahamas."

"When did we get it, grandma?" asked Ned.

"In 1819, by a treaty between the United States and Spain."

"Then the fighting stopped, I suppose?"

"No, Ned. The Seminole Wars followed, lasting between 1835 to 1842. Florida was admitted into the Union in 1845, seceded in 1861, bore her part bravely and well through the Civil War, and at its close, a State Convention repealed the ordinance of secession."

"So since that she has been a part of our Union like the rest of our states. Hasn't she, grandma?" asked Ned.

"Yes, a part of our own dear country—a large and beautiful state."

"It probably will not be long now till some of us, at least, will see her," observed Gracie with obvious satisfaction at that prospect.

"How soon will the *Dolphin* be ready, papa?"

"By the time we are," replied the captain, "which will be as soon as Max can join us."

"Dear Max! I long for the time when he will be with us again," said Violet.

"I suppose by this time he knows how to manage a vessel almost as well as you do, papa?" observed Ned in an inquiring tone.

"I hope so," his father replied with a smile.

"So the passengers may all feel very safe, then, I suppose," said Mrs. Lilburn.

"And that being the case, you are willing to be one of them, Cousin Annis, are you not?" queried Violet hospitably.

"More than willing. We are glad and grateful to you and the captain for the invitation to be counted among them, as my husband is also, I know."

"I am neither able nor desirous to deny that, my dear," laughed Cousin Ronald. "Ah ha, Ah ha, Um hm! It will be my first visit to Florida, and I'm thinking we'll have a grand time of it—looking up the sites and scenes of the old histories we've been reading and chatting over."

CHAPTER SIXTH

THE YACHT WAS READY in due season, and the weather being favorable, Captain Raymond invited as many of the connection as could be comfortably accommodated on board to go with him to witness the graduation of Max and his classmates. Certainly his own immediate family, Mr. and Mrs. Dinsmore, and Grandma Elsie would be of that number. Evelyn Leland and Cousins Ronald and Annis Lilburn were also invited.

Max's joy in meeting them all—especially his father and the others of his own immediate family—was evidently great, for it was the first sight he had had of any of them for two years or more. He passed his examination successfully, received his diploma, and was appointed to the engineer corps of the navy. He received many warm congratulations and valuable gifts from friends and relatives, but the pleasure in his father's eyes, accompanied by the warm, affectionate clasp of his hand and his look of parental pride in his firstborn, was a sweeter reward to the young man than all else put together.

"You are satisfied with me, father?" he asked in a low aside.

"Entirely so, my dear boy," was the prompt and smiling rejoinder. "You have done well and made me a proud and happy father. And now, if you are quite ready for the homeward-bound trip, we will go aboard the yacht at once."

"I am entirely ready, sir," responded Max in very joyful tones. "Trunk packed, and good-byes said."

But they were detained for a little, some of Captain Raymond's old friends coming up to congratulate him and his son on the latter's successful entrance into the most desirable corps of the navy. Then, on walking down to the wharf, they found the *Dolphin's* dory waiting for them and saw that the rest of their party was already on board, on deck and evidently looking with eager interest for their coming.

Max remarked it with a smile, adding, "How the girls have grown, father! And how lovely they all are! Girls that any fellow might be proud to claim as his sisters—and friend. Evelyn, I suppose, would hardly let me claim her as a sister."

"I don't know," laughed his father, "she once very willingly agreed to a proposition from me to adopt her as my daughter."

"Yes? I think she might well be glad enough to do that. But to take me for a brother would not perhaps be quite so agreeable."

"Well, your Mamma Vi objecting to having so old a daughter, we agreed to consider ourselves brother and sister. So I suppose you can consider her your aunt, if you wish."

"There now, father, what a ridiculous idea!" laughed Max.

"Not so very," returned his father, "since aunts are sometimes younger than their nephews."

But they had reached the yacht now, and their conversation went no farther. In another moment, they were on deck, and all the dear relatives and friends were there crowding about Max to tell of their joy in having him in their midst again and in knowing that he had so successfully finished his course of tuition and fully entered upon the profession chosen as his life's work.

Max, blushing with pleasure, returned hearty thanks and expressed his joy in being with them again. "The two years of absence have seemed a long time to be without sight of your dear faces," he said. "I feel it a very great pleasure to be with you all again."

"And it will be a delight to get home once more, won't it?" asked Gracie, hanging lovingly on her brother's arm.

"Indeed it will," he responded. "Getting aboard the dear, old yacht seems like a long step in that direction, particularly as all the family and so many other of my dear friends are here to welcome me."

"Well, we're starting," said Ned. "The sailors have lifted anchor, and we begin to move down stream even now."

At that, silence fell upon the company, all gazing upon the wintry landscape and the vessels lying at anchor in the river as they passed them one after another. But a breeze had sprung up, the air was too cool for comfort, and presently all went below.

Then came the call to the table, where they found an abundance of good cheer awaiting them. The meal was enlivened by much cheerful chat, Max doing his full share of it in reply to many questions in regard to his experiences during the two years of his absence, especially of the last few weeks in which he had not been heard from except in a rather hurried announcement of his arrival at Annapolis. They were all making much of this fine young fellow, but, as his father noticed with great pleasure, it did not seem to spoil him. His manner and speech were modest and unassuming, and he listened with quiet respect to the remarks and queries of the older people. The younger ones were quiet listeners to all.

At the conclusion of the meal, all withdrew to the salon, and the younger ones collected in a group by themselves. Max, seated near to Evelyn Leland, turned to her and in a grave and quiet tone remarked, "It seems a long time since we have had a bit of chat together, Aunt Evelyn."

At that her eyes opened wide in astonishment.

"Aunt?" she repeated. "Why—why, Max, what do you mean by calling me that?"

"I supposed it was the proper title for my father's sister," he returned with a twinkle of fun in his eye.

"Oh!" she laughed. "I had nearly forgotten that bargain made with the captain so long ago. And he has told you of it?"

"Yes. It was in answer to a remark of mine stating that I should like to include you among my sisters. But can you hold that relationship to my father and to me at the same time?"

"That is a question to be carefully considered," she laughed. "In the meantime suppose you just go back to the old way of calling me simply Evelyn or Eva. And shall I call you Max, as of old?"

"Yes, yes, indeed! It's a bargain! And now, girls," glancing from her to his sisters, "as I haven't heard from home in some weeks, perhaps you may have some news to tell me. Has anything happened? Or is anything out of the usual course of events likely to happen?"

At that Gracie laughed; Lucilla blushed and smiled; and little Ned burst out in eager, joyful tones, "Oh, yes, brother Max! Papa is going to take us all to Florida in a day or two, you as well as the rest."

"Indeed!" exclaimed Max. "That will be very pleasant, I think."

"Yes," continued Neddie, "it's because Cousin Dr. Arthur says Chester must go to get cured of his bad cough that he's had so long. Of course, Lu must go if he does—Cousin Chester, I mean—and if Lu goes the rest of us ought to go, too. Don't you think so, brother Max?"

Max's only reply for the moment was a puzzled look from one to another.

"You may as well know it at once, Max," Lucilla said with a smile. "Chester and I are engaged, and naturally he wants us all with him."

"Is it possible?" exclaimed Max, giving her a look of surprise and interest. "Why, Lu, I thought father was quite determined to keep his daughters single until they were far beyond your present age."

"Yes," she returned with a smile. "But I suppose circumstances alter cases. Chester saved my life, Max, at nearly the expense of his own," she added with a tremble in her voice. "So father let him tell me what he had been wanting to, and he has also allowed us to become engaged. But that is to be all, for a year or more."

"Saved your life, Lu? Tell me about it. Please do, for I haven't heard the story."

"You remember the anger of the burglar whom you and I testified against some years ago and his threat to be revenged on me?"

"Yes. In one of father's letters, I was told that he had escaped from prison. And he attacked you?"

"Yes. He fired at me from some bushes by the roadside, but he missed. Chester, who was riding with me, backed up our horses just in time. Then the two of them fired simultaneously at each other, and the convict fell dead. Chester was terribly wounded, while I escaped unhurt. But I thought father had written you all about it."

"If so that letter must have missed me," said Max. "And Chester hasn't recovered entirely?"

"Not quite. His lungs seem weak, but we are hoping that a visit to Florida will perfect his cure."

"I hope so, indeed! I have always liked Chester and shall welcome him as a brother-in-law, since he has saved my sister's life and won her heart."

"And that of her father," added the captain, coming up at that moment and laying a hand on Lucilla's shoulder while he looked down at her with eyes of love and pride. "He has certainly proved himself worthy of the gift of her hand."

"I think I must have missed one of your letters, father," said Max. "Surely you did not intend to keep me in ignorance of all this?"

"No, my son. I wrote you a full account of all but the engagement, leaving that to be told by your sister upon your arrival here. One or more of my recent letters must have missed you."

"Too bad!" exclaimed Max. "For a letter from my father, or from any one of the home folks, is a great treat when I am far away on shipboard or on some distant shore."

"Max, we also feel it a great treat when one comes from you," said Gracie.

"Ah! that's very good of you all," he returned with a pleased smile. "But I think we may look forward to a fine time for the next few weeks or months, as we expect to spend them together."

"Yes," said his father. Then he asked, "Are you well up in the history of Florida, my son?"

"Not so well as I should like to be, sir," returned Max. "But perhaps I can refresh my memory and also learn something new on that subject, while we are on the way there."

"Yes. We have a good supply of books in that line, which we will carry along for your benefit and to perhaps refresh our own memories occasionally. Possibly the girls may like to recount to you some of the tales of early times in that part of the country, which have interested them of late," the captain continued with a smiling glance at Evelyn and his daughters. All three at once and heartily expressed their entire willingness to do so, and Max returned his thanks with the gallant remark that that would be even more delightful than reading the accounts for himself.

"Papa, can't we keep right on now to Florida?" asked Ned.

"No, my son. There are several reasons why that is not practicable—matters to be attended to at home, luggage to be brought aboard the yacht, and so forth. Besides, your brother no doubt wants a sight of Woodburn before setting out upon a journey that is likely to keep us away from there for some weeks."

"Yes, indeed, father, you are right about that," said Max. "I have always esteemed my Woodburn home a lovely and delightful place and dare say I shall find it even more beautiful now than when I saw it last."

"Then we'll expect to hear you say so when you get there," said Lucilla with a smile of pleasure and assurance up into her brother's face.

And she was not disappointed. When at length Woodburn was reached, Max's admiration and delight were evident and fully equal to her expectations. But of necessity, his stay at this time must be brief, scarcely allowing opportunity to see all the relatives and connections residing in that neighborhood if he would not miss having a share in the contemplated trip to Florida.

CHAPTER SEVENTH

THE *DOLPHIN* CARRIED the very same party to Florida that she had brought to and from Annapolis with the addition of Chester Dinsmore and Dr. Harold Travilla, while some others of the connection were intending to travel thither by land. The voyage was but a short one and the weather pleasant, though cool enough to make the cabin a more comfortable place for family gatherings than the deck. The vessel was in fine condition, well manned, well officered, and provided with everything necessary for convenience, comfort, and enjoyment. Amusements—such as music, books, and games—were always to be had in abundance aboard the yacht, but on this occasion the collection of information in regard to the history and geography of Florida took precedence over everything else. As soon as the vessel was well under way, they gathered about a table in the salon upon which were maps and books bearing upon the subject. While examining them, all chatted freely and merrily in regard to which points they should visit and how long to remain in each place.

"That last is a question that would better be decided upon the spot," Captain Raymond said when it had been asked once or twice. "There is little or nothing to hurry us, so that we may move forward or tarry in one place or another, as suits our convenience or inclination."

"We will call at Jacksonville, I suppose, father?" Lucilla said inquiringly. "I see it is spoken of as the travel center and metropolis of the state."

"Yes. If my passengers desire to go there, we will do so."

"Can we go all the way in the *Dolphin*, papa?" asked little Elsie.

"Yes. I think, however, we will call at Fernandina first, as it is nearer."

"It is on an island. Is it not?" asked Evelyn.

"Yes, Amelia Island at the mouth of St. Mary's River, Eva."

"There are a very great many islands on Florida's coast, I think," said Elsie. "I was looking at the map today, and it seemed to me there were thousands."

"So there are," said her father, "islands of various sizes from a mere dot in some cases to thirty or fifty miles of length in others."

"Then we won't stop at all of them, I suppose," remarked Ned sagely, "only at the big ones. Won't we, papa?"

"Yes, and not at every one of them, either," answered his father with a look of amusement. "Ten thousand or more stoppages would use up rather too much of our time."

"Yes, indeed!" laughed Ned. "Most of them I'd rather just look at as we pass by."

"We will want to see St. Augustine and other places mentioned in the histories we have been reading," said Gracie.

"Certainly," replied her father. "We will not neglect them. The mouth of the St. John's River is about the first we will come to. Do you remember, Elsie, what they called it, and what they did there?"

"Oh, yes, papa," she answered eagerly. "They named the river May and set up a monument of stone on a little sand bank in the river and engraved the arms of France upon it."

"Quite correct, daughter," the captain said in a tone of pleased commendation. "I see you have paid good attention to our reading and talks on the subject, and I hope soon to reward you with a sight of the scenes of the occurrences mentioned. Though, of course, they are greatly changed from what they were nearly four hundred years ago."

"Wasn't Jacksonville formerly known by another name, captain?" asked Evelyn.

"Yes," he replied, "the Indian name was Waccapilatka, meaning Cowford or Oxford, but in 1816 it became a white man's town. In 1822, its name was changed to Jacksonville in honor of General Andrew Jackson. I think we should go up the St. John's to that city before going any farther down the coast."

"Yes," said Mrs. Travilla, "and then on up the river and through the lakes to de Leon Springs. We all want to see that place."

All in the company seemed to approve of that plan, and it was presently decided to carry it out. They did not stop at Fernandina, only gazed upon it in passing, made but a short stay at Jacksonville, then passed on up the river and through the lakes to de Leon Springs.

Here they found much to interest them, the great mineral spring—one hundred feet in diameter and thirty feet deep, its water so clear that the bottom could be distinctly seen and so impregnated with soda and sulfur as to make it most healthful, giving ground to the legend that it is the veritable Fountain of Perpetual Youth sought out by Ponce de Leon.

The ruins of an old Spanish mill close at hand interested them also. These consisted of an immense brick smokestack and furnace covered with vines and two large iron wheels that had been thrown down when the mill was destroyed in a way to cause one to overlap the other. Now a gum tree grows up through them so that the arms of the wheels are deeply imbedded in its trunk.

These friends found this so charming a spot that they spent some days there. Then returning down the river to the ocean, they continued their voyage in a southerly direction.

Their next pause was at St. Augustine, which they found a most interesting old city—the oldest in the United States. It is noted for its picturesque beauty, its odd streets ten to twenty feet wide without sidewalks, its crumbling old city gates, its governor's palace, its coquina-built houses with overhanging balconies, its sea walls and old fort, its Moorish cathedral, and the finest and most striking hotel in the world.

But what interested the party more than anything else was the old fort—called San Marco by the Spaniards but now bearing the American name of Fort Marion. They went together to visit it and were greatly interested in its ancient and foreign appearance, the dried-up moat, the drawbridges, the massive arched entrance, the dark under-ways, and the dungeons.

"Papa," said Elsie, "it's a dreadful place, and it is very, very old. Isn't it?"

"Yes," he answered. "It was probably begun in 1565. About how long ago was that?"

"More than three hundred years," she returned after a moment's thought. "Oh, that is a long, long while, papa!"

"Yes," he said, "a very long while, and we may be thankful that our lives were given us in this time rather than in that. For it was a time of ignorance and persecution."

"Yes, yes, ignorance and persecution," the words came in sepulchral tones from the depths of the nearest dungeon. "Here I have lain for three hundred years with none to pity or help. Oh, 'tis a weary while! Shall I never, never escape?"

"Oh, papa," cried Elsie in tones of affright, and clinging to his hand, "how dreadful! Can't we help him out?"

"I don't think there is anyone in there, daughter," the captain said in reassuring tones.

Her Uncle Harold added with a slight laugh, "And if there is, he must surely be pretty used to it by this time."

All their little company had been startled at first and felt a thrill of horror at thought of such misery, but now they all laughed and turned to Cousin Ronald, as if saying surely it was his doing.

"Yes," he said, "the voice was mine. Thankful we may be that those poor victims of such hellish cruelty have long since been released from their pain."

"Oh, I am glad to know that," exclaimed Elsie with a sigh of relief. "But please let's go away from here, for I think it's a dreadful place."

"Yes," said her father, "we have seen it all now and will try to find something more pleasant to look at, my little daughter." And with that they turned and left the old fort.

Captain Raymond and his little company, feeling in no haste to continue their journey, lingered for some time in St. Augustine and its neighborhood. One day, they visited an island where some friends were boarding. It was a very pretty place. There were several cottages standing near together amid the orange groves—one of them occupied by the proprietor, a finely educated Austrian physician, and his wife, the others by the boarders. The party from the *Dolphin* were much interested in the story of these people told them by their friends.

"The doctor," he said, "had come over to America before our Civil War, and he was on the island when Union troops came into the neighborhood. He was one day walking in the woods when suddenly a party of Union soldiers appeared and, seeing him, took him for a spy, seized him, and declared their intention to shoot him. They tied his hands behind his back, led him to what they deemed a suitable spot on the edge of a thick part of the wood, then turned and walked away to station themselves at the proper distance for firing. But the instant their eyes were off him, the prisoner started into the wood and was out of sight before they were aware that he was making an attempt to escape.

"They pursued, but favored by the thick growth of trees and shrubs, he kept out of sight until he reached a palmetto. He climbed this tree, having contrived to get his hands free as he ran, and there concealed himself among the fronds. He had hardly ensconced himself there before he could see and hear his foes running past beneath his place of shelter, beating about the bushes and calling to each other to make sure of catching the rascally spy. But he was safely hidden, and at length they gave up the search for the time.

"But they had encamped in the neighborhood, and for several days and nights the Austrian remained in the tree—afraid to descend lest he should be caught and shot. He did not starve, as he could eat of the cabbage that grows at the top of that tree, but he suffered from thirst and lack of sleep, as he could rest but insecurely in the treetop. When two or three days and nights had passed, he felt that he could stand it no longer. He must get water and food though at the risk of his life. Waiting only for darkness and a silence that led him to hope his foes were not near at hand, he descended and cautiously made his way through the wood. He presently reached a house occupied by a woman only, told her his story, and asked for food and drink. Her heart was touched with pity for his hard case, and she supplied his wants and told him she would put food in a certain spot where he could get it the next night.

"He thanked her and told her he wanted to get away from that neighborhood, as there was no safety for him there. She said she thought she might be able to secure a skiff in which he could go up or down the coast and so perhaps escape the soldiers. He was, you know, a physician—not a sailor—and knew but little about managing a boat. But anything seemed better than his present situation, so he thanked her and said he would be glad to try it.

Shortly afterward, she informed him that the boat was ready. He entered it, took up the oars, and started down the coast. But a storm came on; he was unable to manage his small craft; it was upset by the waves; he was thrown into the water and presently lost consciousness. When he recovered it, he was lying in a berth on board a much larger vessel than the canoe, a kindly looking man leaning over him using restoratives. 'Ah, doctor,' he said with a pleased smile, 'I am glad, very glad to have succeeded in restoring you to consciousness and glad to have been able to rescue you from a watery grave.'

"The doctor expressed his thanks, but he acknowledged that he did not know this new friend, who seemed to know him. The other asked if he did not remember having prescribed for a sick man in such a time and at such a place. 'It was I,' he added. 'You then saved my life, and I am most happy to have been enabled to save yours from being lost in the ocean.'

"The talk went on. The doctor told of his danger, his escape, and his anxiety to keep out of the way of the soldiers until the war should be over.

"The captain told him he was bound for Philadelphia, and that, if he chose, he could go there and live in safety to the end of the war and longer. So that was what he did. He stayed there till peace came, and in the meantime, he met and married a countrywoman of his own, a lovely and amiable lady, whom he brought back with him to Florida."

"I noticed her as we passed," said Grandma Elsie. "She is a lovely-looking woman. But have they no children?"

"None now. They had two—both a son and a daughter—who lived to grow up. They were both children to be proud of, highly educated by their father, and very fond of each other and of their parents. The son used to act as a guide to visitors boarding here in the cottages, going with them on fishing expeditions and so forth. On one of those occasions, he was caught in a storm and took cold. That led to consumption, and he finally died. They buried him under the orange trees. His sister was so overwhelmed with grief that she fretted herself to death, and she now lies by his side."

"Ah, the poor mother!" sighed Grandma Elsie.

"And the father, too," added Captain Raymond in a moved tone.

CHAPTER EIGHTH

Leaving St. Augustine, the *Dolphin* pursued her way down the Florida coast, pausing here and there for a day or two at the most attractive places, continuing on to the southernmost part of the state, going around it past Cape Sable and out into the Gulf of Mexico. Then, having accepted an invitation from Grandma Elsie to visit Viamede, they sailed on in a westerly direction.

They had pleasant weather during their sojourn in and about Florida, but as they entered the Gulf, a rainstorm came up and continued until they neared the port of New Orleans. That confined the women and children pretty closely to the cabin, and active little Ned grew very weary of it.

"I wish I could go on deck," he sighed on the afternoon of the second day. "I'm so tired of staying down here where there's nothing to see."

As he concluded, a voice that sounded like that of a boy about his own age and seemed to come from the stairway to the deck, said, "I'm sorry for that little chap. Suppose I come down there and try to get up a bit of fun for him."

"By all means," replied the captain. "We will be happy to have you do so."

Ned straightened himself up and looked eagerly in the direction of the stairway.

"Who is it, papa?" he asked.

"Why, don't you know me?" asked the voice, this time seeming to come from the door of one of the staterooms down the hall.

"No, I don't," returned Ned. "I didn't know there was any boy on board, except myself."

"Nor did I," said a rough man's voice. "What are you doing here, you young rascal? Came aboard to steal, did you?"

"Nothing but my passage, sir. I'm not doing a bit of harm," replied the boyish voice.

"Oh, I guess I know who you are," laughed Ned. "At least I'm pretty sure you're either Cousin Ronald or brother Max."

At that a loud guffaw right at his ear made the little boy jump with an outcry, "Who was that?"

"Why didn't you look and see?" laughed Lucilla.

"Why, it doesn't seem to have been anybody," returned Ned, looking around this way and that. "But I'm not going to be frightened, for I just know it's one or the other of our ventriloquists. Now, good sirs, please let's have some more of it, for it's real fun."

"Not much, I should think, after you are in on the secret," said Max.

"It's some, though," said Ned. "Because it seems so real even when you do know—or guess—who it is that's doing it."

"Well, now, I'm glad you are so easily pleased and entertained, little fellow," said the voice from the stateroom door. "Perhaps now the captain will let me pay my fare on the yacht by providing fun for his little son. That oldest one doesn't seem to need any. He gets enough talking with the ladies."

"Oh, do you, brother Max?" asked Ned, turning to him.

"Yes," laughed Max, "it's very good fun."

"Hello!" shouted a voice, apparently from the deck. "Mr. Raymond, sir, better come up here and see that we don't run foul of that big steamer—or she of us."

The captain started to his feet, but Max laughed and said in a mirthful tone, "Never mind, father, it's a false alarm, given for Ned's amusement."

"Please don't scare anybody else to amuse me, brother Max," said Ned with the air of one practicing great self-denial.

"I don't think father was really very badly scared," laughed Lucilla. "We may feel pretty safe with two good naval officers and a skillful crew to look out for threatening dangers and help us to avoid them."

"That's right, miss. There's no occasion for anxiety or alarm," said the man's rough voice that had spoken before.

"Thank you. I don't feel a particle of either," laughed Lucilla.

"And I am sure neither you nor any of us should, under the care of two such excellent and skillful seamen," added Violet in a sprightly tone.

"That's right, and I reckon you may feel pretty safe—all o' you," said the man's voice.

"Of course. Who's afraid?" cried the boyish voice, close at Ned's side. "Some of those old Spaniards were drowned in this gulf, but that was because they knew nothing about managing a vessel."

"Oh, yes!" exclaimed Ned. "But my father does know how, and so does brother Max."

"That's a mighty good thing," said the voice. "So, we needn't fear shipwreck, but we can just devote ourselves to having a good time."

"So we can," said Ned. "And we do have good times when papa is at the head of affairs."

"Quite a complimentary speech from my little son," laughed the captain.

"And where are you going in this *Dolphin*?" asked the voice.

"To New Orleans, then to Berwick Bay, and on through the lakes and bayous to my grandma's place—Viamede. I've been there before, and it's very beautiful."

"Then I'd like to go, too," said the voice. "Won't you take me along?"

"Yes, yes, indeed! Whether you are Cousin Ronald or brother Max, I know grandma will make you welcome."

At that everybody laughed, and his grandma said, "Yes, indeed, they are both heartily welcome."

"Whichever you are, I'm much obliged to you for making this fun for me," continued Ned. "Oh, what was that!" as a loud whistle was heard seemingly close behind him. He turned hastily about, then laughed as he perceived that there was no one there. "Was it you, brother Max?" he asked.

"Did it sound like my voice?" asked Max.

"As much as like any other. But oh, there's the call to supper, and I suppose the fun will have to stop for this time."

"Yes, you can have the fun of eating instead," said his father, leading the way to the table.

In due time the next day they reached New Orleans, where they paused for a few days of rest and sightseeing. Then returning to their yacht, they passed out into the Gulf, up the bay into Teche Bayou and beyond, through lake and lakelet, past plain and forest, plantation and swamp. The scenery was beautiful. There were miles and miles of smoothly shaven and velvety green lawns shaded by magnificent oaks and magnolias. There were cool, shady dells carpeted with a rich growth of flowers, lordly villas peering through groves of orange trees, tall white sugar-houses, and long rows of cabins for the laborers. The scenes were not entirely new to anyone on the boat, but they were scarcely the less enjoyable for that—so great was their beauty.

When they reached their destination and the boat rounded to at the wharf, they perceived a welcoming group awaiting their landing—all the relatives from Magnolia, the Parsonage, and Torriswood. There was a joyful exchange of greetings with them and then with the group of servants standing a little in the rear.

In accordance with written directions sent by Grandma Elsie some days in advance of her arrival, a feast had been prepared, and the whole connection in that neighborhood invited to partake of it. And not one older or younger had failed to come, for she was too dearly loved for an invitation from her to be neglected unless the hindrance was such as could not be ignored or set aside. Dr. Dick Percival and his Maud were there among the rest, Dick's half brother Dr. Robert Johnson, and Maud's sister Sydney also. They gave a very joyful and affectionate greeting to their brother Chester and to Lucilla Raymond and attached themselves to her for the short walk from the wharf to the house.

"Oh, Lu," said Maud, "we are so glad that we are to have you for our sister. I don't know any other girl I should be so pleased to have come into the family. And Ches will make a good, kind husband, I am sure. He has always been a dear, good brother."

"Indeed he has," said Sydney. "We have been hoping that he and Frank will come and settle down here near us."

"Oh, no, indeed!" exclaimed Lulu. "I should like to live near you two, but nothing would induce me to make my home so far away from my father. And Chester has promised never to take me away from him."

"Oh, I was hoping you would want to come," said Maud. "But Ches is one to keep his word. So that settles it."

They had reached the house, and here the talk ended for the time.

The new arrivals retired to their rooms for a time to freshen up, and then all gathered about the well-spread board and made a hearty meal. It was enlivened by cheerful chat mingled with many an innocent jest and not a little mirthful laughter. It was still early when the meal was concluded, and the next hour or two were spent in pleasant, familiar interaction upon the verandas or throughout the beautiful grounds. Then the guests began to return to their homes, those with young children leaving first. The Torriswood family stayed a little longer, and at their urgent request Chester consented to become their guest for the first few days, if no longer.

"There are two good reasons why you should do so," said Dick in a half-jesting tone. "Firstly, having married your sister, we are by that way the most nearly related, and secondly, as Bob and I are both physicians, we may be better able to take proper care of you than these good and kind relatives."

"Dick, Dick," remonstrated Violet, "how you have forgotten! Or is it professional jealousy? Have we not been ever so careful to bring along with us one of the very physicians who have had charge of Chester's case?"

"Why, sure enough!" exclaimed Dick. "Harold, old fellow, I beg your pardon! And to make amends, should I get sick, I shall certainly have you called in at once."

"Which will quite make amends," returned Harold, laughingly. "It will give me a good opportunity to punish your impertinence in ignoring my claims as one of the family physicians."

"Ah!" returned Dick. "I perceive that my wiser plan will be to keep well."

There was a general laugh, a moment's pause, then Robert, sending a smiling glance in Sydney's direction, said, "Now, dear friends and relatives, Syd and I have a communication to make. We have decided to follow the good example set us by our brother and sister—Maud and Dick—and so we expect in two or three weeks to take each other for better or for worse."

The announcement caused a little surprise to most of those present, but everyone seemed pleased, thinking it a suitable match in every way.

"I think you have chosen wisely—both of you," said Grandma Elsie. "I hope there are many years of great happiness in store for you—happiness and usefulness. And, Chester," turning to him, "remember that these doors are wide open to you at all times. Come back when you will and stay as long as you will."

"Thank you, cousin. As usual, you are most kindly hospitable," Chester said with a gratified look and smile. "The two places are so very near together that I can readily divide my time between them, which—both being so attractive—is certainly very fortunate for me."

"And for all of us," said Violet. "We shall be able to see more of each other than we could if we were situated farther apart."

"Yes. I shall hope and expect to see you all coming to call every day," added her mother with hospitable cordiality.

"Thank you, Cousin Elsie," said Maud. "But, though it is delightful to come here, we must not let it be altogether a one-sided affair. Please remember to return our visits whenever you find it convenient and pleasant to do so."

With that they took leave and departed, and a little later those constituting the family for the time bade each other goodnight, and most of them retired to their sleeping apartments.

Not quite all of them, however, retired early. Max, Evelyn, and Lucilla stepped out upon the veranda again. Max remarked, "The grounds are looking bewitchingly beautiful in the moonlight. Suppose we take a little stroll down to the bayou."

"You two go if you like, but I want to have a word or two with papa," said Lucilla, glancing toward her father, who was standing quietly and alone at some little distance, seemingly absorbed in gazing upon the beauties of the landscape.

"Well, we will not be gone long," said Evelyn, as she and Max descended the steps while Lucilla glided softly in her father's direction.

He did not seem aware of her approach until she was close at his side, and laying a hand on his arm, she said in her low, sweet tones, "I have come for my dear father's goodnight caresses and to hear anything he may have to say to his eldest daughter."

"Ah, that is right," he said, turning and putting an arm about her and drawing her into a close embrace. "I hope all goes well with you, dear child. If not, your father is the very one to bring your troubles to."

"Thank you, dear papa," she said. "If I had any troubles I should certainly bring them to you, but I have not. Oh, I do think I am the happiest girl in the land with your dear love and Chester's, too, having Max with us again, and all of us well and in this lovely, lovely place!"

"Yes, we have a great deal to be thankful for," he returned. "But you will miss Chester, now that he has left here for Torriswood."

"Oh, not very much," she said with her happy, little laugh. "He has assured me that he will be here at least a part of every day, and the ride or walk from Torriswood is not too long to be taken with both pleasure and profit."

"And doubtless some of the time you will be there. By the way, you should give Sydney something very handsome as a wedding present. You may consider what is suitable and likely to please, consult with the other ladies, and let your father know what the decision is—that he may get the article or supply the means."

"Thank you ever so much, father dear," she replied in grateful tones. "But you have given me such a generous supply of pocket money that I don't think I shall need to call upon you for help about this. But I shall ask your advice about what the gift shall be and be sure not to buy anything of which you do not approve."

"Spoken like my own dear, loving daughter," he said approvingly and with a slight caress. "Did Robert Johnson's bit of news make my daughter and her fiancé a trifle jealous that their engagement must be so long a one?"

"Not me, papa. I am entirely willing—yes, very glad—to be subject to your orders and very loath to leave the dear home with you and pass from under your care and protection. Oh, I sometimes feel as if I could never do it. But then I say to myself, 'But I shall always be my dear father's child, and we need not—we will not—love each other the less because another claims a share of my affection.' Is that not so, papa?"

"Yes, daughter, and I do not believe anything can ever make either one of us love the other less. But it is growing late and is about time for my eldest daughter to be seeking her nest, if she wants to be up with the birds in the morning, ready to share a stroll with her father through these beautiful grounds before breakfast."

"Yes, sir. But, if you are willing, I should like to wait for Evelyn. She and Max will be in presently, I think. Papa, I do think they have begun to fall in love, and I am glad. I should dearly love to have Eva for a sister."

"And I should not object to having her for a daughter," returned the captain with a pleased little laugh. "And you are not mistaken in you perception, Lu, so far as Max is concerned. He asked me today if I were willing that he should try to win the dear girl, and I told him most decidedly so and that I heartily wished him success in his wooing. Though, as in your case, I think marriage would be better deferred for a year or two."

"Yes, Max would be quite as much too young for a bridegroom as I for a bride," she said with a slight and amused laugh. "I don't believe he would disregard his father's advice. All your children love you dearly and have great confidence in your opinion on every subject, father dear."

"As I have in their love and willingness to be guided by me," the captain responded in a tone of gratification. "You may wait for Evelyn. I think she and Max will be in presently. Ah, yes. See, they are turning this way now."

꙰ ꙰ ꙰ ꙰ ꙰

Max had given his arm to Evelyn as they left the house, and crossing the lawn together, they strolled slowly down to the bank of the bayou.

"Oh, such a beautiful night it is!" exclaimed Evelyn. "The air is so soft and balmy one can hardly realize that in our more northern homes cold February reigns."

"No," said Max, "and I am glad we are escaping the blustery March winds that will soon be visiting that section. Still, for the year round, I prefer that climate to this."

"Yes, but it is very pleasant to be able to go from one section to another as the seasons change," said Eva. "I think we are very fortunate people in being able to do it."

"Yes," returned Max. "After all, one's happiness depends far more upon being in congenial society and with loved ones than upon climate, scenery, or anything else. Eva," and he turned to her as with sudden determination, "I—I think I can never again be happy away from you. I love you and want you for my own. You have said you would like to be my father's daughter, and I can make you that if you will only let me. Say, dearest—oh, say that you will let me—that you will be mine—my own dear, little wife."

"Max, oh, Max," she answered in low, trembling tones. "I—I am afraid you don't know me quite as I am—that you would be disappointed—would repent of having said what you have just now."

"Never, never! If only you will say yes. If you will only promise to be mine—my own love, my own dear, little wife." And putting an arm about her, he drew her close, pressing an ardent kiss upon her soft lips.

She did not repulse him, and continuing his endearments and entreaties, he at length drew from her an acknowledgment that she returned his love.

Presently they turned their steps back toward the mansion, as happy a pair as could be found in the whole length and breadth of the land.

Captain Raymond and Lucilla were waiting for them, and Max, leading Evelyn to his father, said in joyous tones, "I have won a new daughter for you, father, and a dear, sweet wife for myself. At least she has promised to be both to us one of these days."

"Ah, I am well pleased," the captain said, taking Eva's hand in his and bending down to give her a fatherly caress. "I have always felt that I should like to take her into my family and play a father's part by her."

"Oh, captain, you are very, very kind," returned Eva, low and feelingly. "There is nobody in the wide world whose daughter I should prefer to be."

"Eva, I shall be glad to have you really my sister!" exclaimed Lucilla, giving her friend a warm embrace. "Max, you dear fellow, I'm ever so glad and so much obliged to you."

"You needn't be, sis. Eva is the one deserving of thanks for accepting one so little worthy of her as this sailor brother of yours," returned Max with a happy laugh.

"Yes, we will give her all the credit, my son," said the captain. "I hope that you, my son, will do your best to prove yourself worthy of the prize you have won. And now, my dears, it is high time we were all retiring to rest in order that we may have strength and spirits for the duties and pleasures of tomorrow."

Evelyn and Lucilla were sharing a room at Viamede that communicated directly with the one occupied by Gracie and little Elsie, and that one opened into the one where the captain and Violet slept.

In compliance with the captain's advice, the young girls at once retired to their room to seek their couches for the night. But first they indulged in a bit of loving chat.

"Oh, Eva!" Lucilla exclaimed, holding her friend in a loving embrace. "I am so glad—so very, very glad that we are to be sisters. And Max, I am sure, will make you a good, kind husband. He has always been the best and dearest of brothers to me, as well as to Gracie and the little ones."

"Yes, I know it, Lu," said Evelyn softly. "I know, too, that your father has always been the best and kindest of husbands and that Max is very much like him."

"And you love Max?"

"How could I help it?" asked Evelyn, blushing as she spoke. "I thought it was as a dear brother I cared for him, till—till he asked me to—to be his wife. But then I knew better. Oh, it is so sweet to learn that he loved me so! And I am so happy! I am not the lonely girl I was this morning—fatherless and motherless and without brother or sister. Oh, I have them all now—except the mother," she added with a slight laugh. "For, of course, your Mamma Vi is much too young to be that to me."

"Yes, as she is to be a mother to Max, Gracie, and me. But with such a father as ours, one could do pretty well without a mother. Don't you think so?"

"Yes. He seems to be both father and mother to those of his children who have lost their mother."

"He is, indeed. But now I must obey his last order by getting to bed as quickly as I can."

"I, too," laughed Evelyn. "It seems delightful to have a father to obey." She ended with a slight sigh, thinking of her dear father who had been so long in that better land.

CHAPTER NINTH

LUCILLA AWOKE AT HER usual early hour, rose at once, and moving so quietly about as not to disturb Evelyn's slumbers, she attended to all the duties of the time and went softly from the room and down to the front veranda, where she found her father pacing slowly to and fro.

"Ah, daughter," he said, holding out his hand with a welcoming smile, "good morning. I am glad to see you looking bright and well," and drawing her into his arms, he gave her his usual welcoming caress.

"As I feel, papa," she returned. "I hope you, too, are quite well."

"Yes, entirely so. It is a lovely morning, and I think we will find a stroll along the bank of the bayou very enjoyable. However, I want you to eat a bit of something first. Here is Aunt Phillis with oranges prepared in the usual way for an early morning treat," he added as she stepped from the doorway bearing a small silver waiter upon which a dish of oranges was ready for eating.

"Yes, sah, Captain. I hope you, sah, and Miss Lu kin eat what's heah. Dere's plenty moah for de res' ob de folks when dey gets out o' dere beds."

"Yes," said the captain, helping them both. "There is always an abundance of good cheer where your Miss Elsie is at the head of affairs."

"Father," Lucilla said as they set off across the lawn after eating the oranges, "I am so pleased that Max and Eva are engaged. I should prefer her for a sister-in-law to anyone else. I have always loved her dearly since we first met."

"Yes, I can say the same. She is a dear girl, and Max could have done nothing to please me better," was the captain's answering remark.

"And she loves you, father," returned Lucilla, smiling up into his eyes, "which, of course, seems very strange to me."

"Ah? Although I know you to be guilty of the very same thing yourself," he returned with an assured smile, pressing affectionately the hand he held in his.

"Ah, but having been born your child, how can I help it?" she asked with a happy little laugh. Then she went on, "Father, I've been thinking how it might do for you to make the house you have been talking of building near your own big enough for two families—Max and Eva's, Chester's and mine."

"Perhaps that might do," he answered pleasantly. "But it is hardly at all necessary to consider the question yet."

"No, sir," she returned. "Oh, I am glad I do not have to leave my sweet home in my father's house for months or maybe years yet. I do so love to be with you that I don't know how I can ever feel willing to leave you—even for Chester, whom I do really love very dearly."

"And I shall find it very hard to have you leave me," he said. "But we expect to be near enough to see almost as much of each other as we do now."

"Yes, papa, that's the pleasant part of it," she said with a joyous look. Then she went on, "Chester has been talking to me about plans for the house, but I tell him that, as you said just now, it is hardly time to think about them yet."

"There would be no harm in doing so, however," her father said, "and no harm in deciding just what you would like before work on it is begun. I should like to make it an ideal home for my dear, eldest daughter and her husband."

"Thank you, father dear," she said. "I do think you are just the most kind father anyone ever had."

"I have no objection to your thinking so," he returned with a pleased smile. He then went on to speak of some plans for the building that had occurred to him. "We will examine the plans," he said, "and try to think in what respect each might be improved. I intend for my daughter's home to be as convenient, cozy, and comfortable as possible. You must not hesitate to suggest improvements that may occur to you."

"Thank you, papa. How good and kind you are to me! Oh, I wish I had been a better daughter to you—never willful or disobedient."

"Dear child, you are a great comfort to me and have been for years past," he said. He then went on to speak more of the plans that he had been considering for the new home to be constructed upon his property.

In the meantime, they had walked some distance along the bank of the bayou, and glancing at his watch, the captain said it was time to return, as it was not far from the breakfast hour, and that they would most likely find some, if not all, of the others ready for and awaiting the summons to the table.

☙ ☙ ☙ ☙ ☙

Lucilla had scarcely left her sleeping apartment when Eva awoke, and seeing that the sun was shining, she arose and made quick work of dressing—carefully, though, thinking of Max and his interest in her—that it should be neat and becoming.

She descended the stairs as the captain and Lucilla were approaching the house on their return from their walk. Max was waiting on the veranda while most of the other guests had gathered in the nearest parlor, and as Eva stepped out upon the veranda, Max came swiftly to meet her.

"My darling!" he said, low and tenderly, putting his arm about her and giving her an ardent kiss. "My own promised one. You are lovelier than ever. A treasure far beyond my deserts, but as you have given your dear self to me, you are mine. Let this seal our compact," slipping upon her finger, as he spoke, a ring set with a very large and brilliant diamond.

"Oh, how lovely!" she exclaimed, looking at it and lifting to his face eyes filled with love and joy. "It is very beautiful, dear Max, and valuable for that reason, but it is still more so for being the emblem of your dear love—love that makes me the happiest girl in the land."

"As yours makes me the happiest man. Ah, Eva dear, I am not worthy of you."

She laughed, "I shall take your opinion on most subjects, but not on that one. Here comes your father and Lulu."

"Good morning," they said together, coming up the steps.

The captain added in jesting tones, "Ah, Max, my son, you seem to be making an early return to the business begun yesterday."

"Something more, captain," Eva said, displaying his gift. "Is it not lovely?"

"Oh, how beautiful!" exclaimed Lucilla.

"As handsome a diamond as ever I did see," remarked the captain, examining it critically. "But it is none too handsome or expensive for a gift to my new daughter that is to be," he added with a smile, imprinting a kiss upon the small, white hand that wore the ring. "Shall we join the others in the parlor now? And will you let Max tell them of his good fortune? You will, neither of you, surely, wish to keep it a secret from friends so near and dear."

"I do not," said Max. "But it shall be just as you decide, Eva dear," he added in low and tender tones, drawing her within his arms as he spoke.

"I think your—our—father's opinions are always right, Max," she said with a smile and a blush.

"Will you go in first, father? You and Lu, and we will follow," said Max. The captain, at once, taking Lucilla's hand in his, led the way.

"Good morning to you all, friends and relatives," was his cheerfully toned and smiling address as he entered the room, "I hope you are all well and in good spirits."

Then, stepping aside, he allowed Max to pass him with the blushing Evelyn on his arm.

He led her to Mrs. Travilla, saying, "A very good morning to you, Grandma Elsie. I want to introduce you to my future wife. For this dear girl has, to my great joy, promised to become just that one of these days."

"Ah! Is that so, Max? I know of nothing that could please me better," exclaimed that dear lady, rising to her feet and bestowing a warm embrace upon the blushing, happy-faced Evelyn.

Violet was beside them in an instant, exclaiming in joyous tones, "Oh, Eva and Max! How glad I am! I am sure you were made for each other and will be very happy together."

"And are you willing to let me be the captain's daughter?" asked Eva with a charming blush accompanied by a slightly roguish laugh.

"Yes, seeing that Max calls me Mamma Vi, and you are really younger than he," was Violet's laughing reply.

But now Gracie, little Elsie, and the others were crowding around with expressions of surprise and pleasure and many congratulations and good wishes. For everybody who knew them loved both Max and Eva.

The call to breakfast came, and they repaired to the dining room and gathered about the table, as cheerful and merry a party as could be found in the whole land.

"You seem likely to have a rapid increase in your family, captain," said Dr. Harold Travilla with a smiling glance directed toward Lucilla, Max, and Eva, who were all seated near together.

"Some time hence," returned the captain quite pleasantly. "I consider them all young enough to wait a little, and they are dutifully willing to do as I desire."

"As they certainly should be, considering what a good and kind father you are, sir, and how young they are."

"And how pleasant are the days of courtship," added Mr. Lilburn, "as no doubt they will prove with them."

"How wise as well as kind our father is," said Max, giving the captain an ardently appreciative look and smile. "How patiently and earnestly he has striven to bring his children up for usefulness and happiness in this world and the next."

"That is true," said Violet. "I think no one ever had a better father than yours, Max."

"And certainly no one had a more appreciative wife or children than I," remarked Captain Raymond with a smile. "We seem to have formed a mutual admiration society this morning."

"Surely the very best kind of society for families to form among themselves," laughed Harold.

"I like the way our young people are pairing off," remarked Mr. Dinsmore. "The matches arranged from among them seem to be very suitable. By the way, Elsie, we must be planning for some wedding gifts for Bob and Sydney."

"Yes, sir," replied Mrs. Travilla. "I have been thinking of that, but I have not decided upon any particular article yet. I suppose our better plan will be to buy in New Orleans."

"Yes, I think so. It will be well for us all to have consultation on the subject in order to avoid giving duplicates of particular items."

"A good idea, grandpa," said Violet. "There are so many of us — counting the Magnolia and Parsonage people, as well as those of Torriswood. Might it not be well to have that consultation soon to determine what each will give and then set about securing the articles in good season for the wedding, which will probably take place in about three weeks?"

There was a general approval of that idea, and it was decided to take prompt measures for carrying it out.

The meal concluded, all gathered in the family parlor and held the usual morning service of prayer, praise, and reading of the Scriptures. That over, they gathered upon the front veranda and were again engaged in discussing the subject of wedding gifts when Dr. Percival drove up with his wife and her brother. They were most cordially greeted and invited to give their views in regard to the subject that was engaging the thoughts of the others at the moment.

"I think it would be wise for us all to agree as to what each one shall give, so that there will be no duplicates," said Maud.

"Yes," said Violet, "that is the conclusion we have all come to as well."

"Very good," said Maud. "And Sydney wanted me to consult with you older ladies in regard to the material of her wedding dress—whether it should be silk or satin—and about the veil. They are to be married during the morning hours out under the orange trees."

"Oh, that will be lovely," said Violet.

"Yes, I think so. It will allow plenty of room," continued Maud. "And we need plenty because our two doctors want to invite so many of their patients lest somebody should feel hurt by being left out. Our idea is to have the ceremony a little before noon and the wedding breakfast on the lawn immediately following it."

"I like that," said Violet. "As to the wedding dress question, suppose we send to New Orleans for samples and let Sydney choose from them and order the quantity she wants?"

"That strikes me as a very good idea," said Chester. "I want it distinctly understood that I pay for this wedding dress. I had no opportunity to do a brother's part by Maud at the time of her marriage, but I insist that I shall be allowed to do so by this only remaining sister."

"Yes, Chester, you and I will both insist upon being allowed our rights this time," laughed Dick. "Especially as there will be no single sister left to either of us."

"And between you and the other relatives to help, Sydney will fare well, I hope and believe," remarked Mr. Dinsmore with a smile.

"Chester," said Lucilla in a low aside, "I would like your help in choosing my gift for your sister. I have the greatest confidence in your judgment and taste."

"Thank you, dearest," he returned with a pleased smile. "I shall be very glad to give my opinion for what it is worth."

"I presume you have sent or will promptly send word to Frank that his sister is about to marry?" Mr. Dinsmore remarked in a tone between assertion and inquiry.

"We have written," replied Dick. "But we are not at all certain that the letter will reach him in time, as he may have left Florida before it could be received."

"I do not quite despair of getting him here in due season," remarked Chester. "I think we will hear of his whereabouts in time to send him a telegram."

Just at that moment, the Magnolia carriage was seen coming up the driveway with Mr. and Mrs. Embury in it.

They had come to consult with all the Viamede relatives and friends in regard to preparations for the approaching wedding and suitable and desirable gifts for the bride. Mrs. Embury, being sister-in-law to Mrs. Percival and half sister to

Dr. Robert Johnson, felt particularly interested and desirous to do her full share in helping the young couple with their preparations for making a home for themselves.

"Do they intend to go to housekeeping?" she asked of Maud.

"It is hardly decided yet," replied Maud. "We are trying to persuade them that it will be best for us all to continue to be one family. I think that will be the way for the time at least. When we tire of that, we can easily occupy the house as two families. It is large enough and so planned that it can readily be used in that way."

"A very good thing," remarked Mr. Embury. "I think you will be all the more likely to agree if you do not feel that you are shut up to the necessity of remaining one family."

"You have hardly sent out your invitations yet?" Molly said half inquiringly.

"Only to the most distant relatives," replied Maud. "Of course we cannot expect that they will all come, but we did not want to neglect any of them."

"We must arrange to accommodate them if they should come," said Molly. "I hope most of them will. Now about making purchases—of wedding gifts, wedding finery, and so forth. New Orleans will, of course, be our best place for shopping if we want to see the goods before buying. Does anybody feel inclined to go there and attend to the matter?"

There was a silence for a moment. Then Captain Raymond said, "The *Dolphin* and I are at the service of any one—or any number—who would like to go."

Both Maud and Molly thought themselves too busy with home preparations, and after some discussion, it was finally decided that Mrs. Travilla, Violet and the captain, Eva and Max, Lulu and Chester, and Gracie and Harold should form the deputation and that they would go the next Monday morning—this being Saturday. That matter settled, the Emburys and Percivals took their departure.

Then a thought seemed to strike Grandma Elsie. "Annis," she said, turning to her cousin, "cannot you and Cousin Ronald go with us? Please, I wish you would."

"Why, yes. If you want us, I think we can," laughed Annis, turning an inquiring look upon her own husband.

"If you wish it, dear," he answered pleasantly. "I always enjoy being with the cousins." And so it was decided they would be of the party.

CHAPTER TENTH

"Now, my daughters, Lucilla and Gracie, if you have any preparations to make for your trip to new Orleans, my advice is that you attend to them at once," Captain Raymond said when their callers had gone.

"Yes, sir," they both returned, making prompt movement to obey.

Lucilla added, "Though I am sure we have but little to do."

"And what are your directions to me, Captain Raymond? Or am I to be left entirely to my own devices?" laughed Violet.

"I think my wife is wise enough to be safely so left," he replied in his usual pleasant tones. With a look of fond appreciation, he continued, "Perhaps you might give some advice to my daughters," he added.

"Now that I think of it, perhaps it might be well to consult them in regard to some matters," said Violet, and she hurried away after the girls, who had gone up to their sleeping apartments.

"Have not you some preparations to make also, Elsie?" asked Mr. Dinsmore of his daughter.

"Very little," she answered with a smile. "I have only some packing that my maid can do in a few minutes. Ah, here is Uncle Joe to speak to me, I think," as an elderly man came out upon the veranda, bowed to the company in general, then looked toward her with a sort of pleading expression, as if he had a petition to offer.

She rose and went to him, asking in a kindly inquiring tone, "What is it, Uncle Joe?"

"Ise come to ask a favor, mistiss," he replied, bowing low. "Ole Aunt Silvy she mighty porely—mos' likely gwine die befo' many days—an' she doan pear to feel pow'ful sure ob de road for to git to de bes' place on de furder side ob de river. She says Miss Elsie knows da way, and maybe she come and 'struct her how to find it."

"Indeed, I shall be very glad if I can help her to find it," Elsie answered with emotion. "I will go with you at once." Turning to her son, "Harold," she said, "Uncle Joe reports a woman as very ill. Will you come down there with me and see if your medical skill can give her any relief?"

"Certainly, mother," replied Harold, hastening to her side. Excusing herself to her guests and taking her son's arm, Mrs. Travilla at once set off with Uncle Joe following, ready to point out the cabin where the ailing old woman lay.

They found her tossing about upon her bed, moaning and groaning. "Oh, mistiss," she cried as they entered, "you's berry good comin' fo' to see dis po' ole un. I'se pow'ful glad for to see you, mistiss, an' de young doctah, too. Uncle Joe, set out dat cheer fo' de mistiss and dat oder one for de young doctah."

Uncle Joe hastened to do her bidding, while Harold felt her pulse and questioned her in regard to her illness.

She complained of misery in her head, misery in her back, and being "pow'ful weak," finishing up with the query, "Is I gwine die dis day, suh?"

"I think not," he replied. "You may live for weeks or months. But life is very uncertain with us all, and I advise you to promptly make every preparation for death and eternity."

"Dat's what I gwine do when mistiss tell me how," she groaned with a look of keen distress directed toward Mrs. Travilla.

"I will try to make the way plain to you," that lady returned in compassionate tones. "It is just to come to the Lord Jesus confessing that you are a helpless, undone sinner and asking Him to help you and to take away the love of sinning and wash you in His own precious blood. The Bible tells us 'He is able also to save them to the uttermost that come unto God by Him.' And He says, 'Him that cometh to Me I will in no wise cast out.' So that if you come, truly seeking Him with all your heart and truly desiring to be saved, not only from eternal death but from sin and the love of it, He will hear and save you."

"Won' you pray to de good Lawd for me, my sweet mistiss?" pleaded the woman. "You knows bes' how to say de words, an' dis chile foller you in her heart."

At that, Mrs. Travilla knelt beside the bed and offered up an earnest prayer so that the poor, sick woman on the bed could readily feel it all and follow in her heart.

"Dis chile am berry much 'bliged, mistiss," she said when Mrs. Travilla had resumed her seat by the bedside. "I do tink de good Lawd hear dat prayer an open de gate ob heaben to ole Silvy when she git dar."

"I hope so, indeed," Mrs. Travilla replied. "Put your trust in Jesus, and you will be safe. He died to save sinners such as you and I. We cannot do anything to save ourselves, but to all who come to Him He gives salvation without money and without price. Don't think you can do anything to earn it. It is His free gift."

"But de Lawd's chillens got to be good, mistiss, ain't dey?"

"Yes. They are not truly His children if they do not try to know and do all His holy will. Jesus said, 'If ye love Me, keep My commandments.' 'Ye are My friends, if ye do whatsoever I command you.' We have no right to consider ourselves Christians if we do not try earnestly to keep all His commands and do all His holy will."

Harold had sat there listening very quietly to all his mother said and had knelt with her when she prayed. Now, when she paused for a little, he questioned Aunt Silvy about her ailments, gave her directions for taking some medicine, and said he would send it presently from the house. Mrs. Travilla added that she would send some delicacies to tempt the sickly appetite. Then with a few more kindly words, they left the cabin, bidding Uncle Joe a kindly good-bye as they went.

"You do not think Aunt Silvy is really a dying woman, Harold?" his mother said in a tone of inquiry, as they walked on together.

"No, mamma. I shall not be surprised if she lives for a year yet," Harold answered cheerily. "No doubt she is suffering, but I think medicine, rest, and suitable food will relieve her. She will probably be about again in a week or two. But preparations for death and eternity can do her no harm."

"No, certainly. To become a Christian must add to the happiness — as well as safety — of anyone."

"And you have brought that happiness to many a one, my dear mother," Harold said, giving her a tenderly affectionate look. "How often in thinking of you I recall those words of the prophet Daniel, 'And they that be wise shall shine as the brightness of the firmament; and they that turn many to righteousness, as the stars for ever and ever.'"

"'Tis a precious promise," she said with emotion. "Oh, my son, make it the business of your life to do that — to help to the healing of souls, the immortal part, even more than that of the frail bodies that must soon die."

"Yes, mother," he said with emotion. "I do try constantly to do that, and it is a great comfort and help to me to know that my dear mother is often asking help for me from on high."

"Yes," she said. "Without that, none of us could accomplish anything in the way of winning souls for Christ, and every Christian should feel that that is his principal work. This life is so short, and the never-ending ages of eternity are so long. 'Whatsoever thy hand findeth to do, do it with thy might; for there is no work nor device, nor knowledge, nor wisdom in the grave whither thou goest.'"

They walked on in silence for a little. Harold remarked that the air was delightful and an extended walk might prove beneficial to them both.

"Yes let us do just that, son," replied his mother. "Shall we take a stroll through the orange orchard?

The sight and perfume of the fruit and blossoms are delightful this time of year."

"Yes, indeed!" he said. "You can also see, mother, whether everything is properly cared for."

"I expect to find it so," she returned. "I have every reason to believe my manager both faithful and competent."

They enjoyed their stroll greatly, and she found no reason to change her opinion of the manager.

It was lunchtime when they returned to the house, and on leaving the table, some of their party went for a row on the bayou while the rest chose riding or driving through the beautiful woods. Evelyn and Max, Lucilla and Chester formed the riding party and greatly enjoyed their little excursion. The courting of the two young couples was carried on in a very quiet way, but it was none the less satisfactory and enjoyable for that. All four of them felt a great interest in the approaching wedding, and much of their talk as they rode was of it and what gifts to the bride would be the most appropriate and acceptable.

"Chester, you know you have promised to advise me what to give to Sydney," Lucilla said with a smile into his eyes.

"You, dear girl! So I will, and I make that same request of you. For I am sure you know far more about such matters than I do," he returned with a very loving look.

"Quite a mistake, Mr. Dinsmore," she laughed. "But I understood you intended to give some part of the trousseau—perhaps the wedding dress."

"Yes, that and much of all the rest of it. I am sure your help will be quite invaluable in the choice of the various articles."

"Thank you," she said with a pleased laugh. "It is very nice to have you think so highly of my judgment and taste. I hope you will let Grandma Elsie and Mamma Vi and Eva assist in the selection."

"Certainly, if you wish it, but I do not promise to let their opinions have as much weight with me as yours, Lu."

"No, you needn't," she returned merrily. "It is by no means disagreeable to have you consider mine the most valuable, even though it be really worthless in other people's esteem. It is very possible that Sydney might prefer their choice to mine."

"Ah! But she won't have a chance. Your father has a good deal of taste in the line of ladies' dress, has he not?"

"I certainly think so," she returned with a pleased smile. "He has selected many an article of dress for me, and he has always suited my taste as well as if I had been permitted to choose for myself. What he buys is sure to be of excellent quality and suited to the intended wearer's age, complexion, and needs."

"You are very fond of your father," Chester said with a smile.

"Indeed I am," she returned in an earnest tone. "I believe I give him all the love that should have been divided between him and my mother, had she lived. Mamma Vi calls him my idol, but I don't think I make him quite that. He has at least one rival in my affection these days," she added with a blush and in a tone so low that he barely caught the words.

"And may I guess who that is, may I, dearest?" he returned in the same low key and with a look that spoke volumes of love and joy in the certainty of her affection.

Max and Eva, riding on a trifle faster, were just far enough ahead and sufficiently absorbed in their own private chat to miss this little colloquy. There were some love passages between them also and some talk of what they hoped the future held in store for them when they should be old enough for the dear, honored father to give his consent to their immediate marriage. Neither of them seemed to have a thought of going contrary to his wishes, so strong was their affection for him and their faith in his wisdom and his love for them.

All four greatly enjoyed their ride and returned to their temporary home in fine health and spirits.

Chester had rid himself of his troublesome cough before landing in Louisiana, and he was now looking younger and handsomer than he had before that almost fatal wound — a fact that greatly rejoiced the hearts of his numerous relatives and friends. None more so than that of his betrothed, for whose defense he had risked his life.

By the time the Viamede dinner hour had arrived, all the pleasure parties had returned and were ready to do justice to the good cheer provided in abundance. The meal was enlivened by much cheerful chat. The evening was spent much as the previous one had been, and all retired early that Sabbath morning might find them rested, refreshed, and ready for the duties and enjoyments of the sacred day.

CHAPTER ELEVENTH

THE SABBATH MORNING dawned both bright and clear, and as in former days, all of the family, old and young, attended church and the pastor's Bible class. In the afternoon, the house and plantation servants collected on the lawn and were addressed by Captain Raymond and Dr. Harold Travilla. Hymns were sung, too, and prayers offered up to Him from whom all good comes.

The services over, the little congregation slowly dispersed. Some lingered a few minutes for a shake of the hand and a few kind words from their loved mistress, Mrs. Travilla, or her father or son. Then, as the last one turned to depart, the captain and the doctor walked down to the servant's quarters for a short call upon Aunt Silvy, still lying in her bed.

Mrs. Travilla had seated herself on the veranda and seemed to be doing nothing but gazing out upon the lovely landscape—the velvety, flower bespangled lawn, the bayou, the fields, and woods beyond. But the slight patter of little feet drew her attention from that, and turning, she found Elsie and Ned at her side.

"Grandma, would it be disturbing if I talk to you and ask some questions?" asked the little girl.

"No, dear children, not at all," was the kind reply. "I am always glad to help my dear, little grandchildren to information when it is in my power. Here is an empty chair on each side of me. Draw them up closely, you and Ned, and seat yourselves. Then I hope we can have a nice talk."

"Yes, ma'am. It will be a pleasant rest, too," returned the little girl, as she and her brother followed the directions. "Papa told me once that the meaning of the word Sabbath is rest. But what I wanted particularly to ask about this time, grandma, is the Feast of the Passover. Will you please tell us why it was kept and why they called it that?"

"Surely, my dear children, you have heard the story of the institution of that feast of the Jews called the Passover!" said Grandma Elsie in some surprise. "In the twelfth chapter of Exodus there is a full account of its institution. Every household in Israel was to take a lamb of a year old without blemish, and at evening on the fourteenth day of the month it was to be slain. The householder was then to take the blood of the lamb and sprinkle the doorposts of his house. That was to be a sign to the destroying angel, who was to slay the firstborn of the Egyptians that night, not to enter and slay here. Then they were to roast the flesh of the lamb and eat it that night with unleavened bread and bitter herbs. The lives of the Israelites were saved from the angel as it 'passed over,' instead of entering the house to destroy life."

"Oh, yes, grandma. I understand now," said the little girl. "But why is Christ called our passover? You know the verse—'for even Christ our Passover is sacrificed for us.'"

"You know," said her grandmother, "that Jesus is often called the 'Lamb of God.' That paschal lamb symbolized a type of Christ and is so spoken of in Scriptures."

"Thank you, grandma, for telling me," Elsie said gratefully. "And the Jews kept the feast every year from that time till the time of Christ, I suppose. And he kept it, too. Wasn't it at that feast that he instituted what we call the 'Lord's Supper?'"

"Yes," replied her grandmother. "He used the bread and wine that were a part of that feast, saying, '"Take, eat; this is my body." And He took the cup and gave thanks, and gave it to them, saying, "Drink ye all of it; for this is my blood of the New Testament, which is shed for many for the remission of sins."'"

"Oh, grandma, how good and kind He was to shed His blood for us! To die that dreadful, dreadful death of the cross that we might go to heaven!" exclaimed the little girl with tears in her sweet blue eyes. "I do love Him for it, and I want to be His servant, doing everything He would have me to do."

"That is how we all should feel, dear child," replied her grandmother, bending down to press a kiss upon the rosy cheek.

"I do, grandma," said Ned. "Do you think the Lord Jesus takes notice that we love Him and want to do as He tells us?"

"Yes, Neddie dear, I am quite sure of it," replied his grandmother. "The Psalmist says, 'Thou compassest my path and my laying down, and art acquainted with all my ways. For there is not a word in my tongue, but, lo, oh, Lord, thou knowest it altogether.'"

"It is so good, grandma, that God doesn't think us not even worth noticing," said Elsie. "I'm so very glad that He sees and cares for us all the time and lets us ask His help whenever we will ask it of Him."

"It is indeed good, my child, and we are sure of it. Jesus said, 'Are not two sparrows sold for a farthing? And one of them shall not fall to the ground without your Father. But the very hairs of your head are all numbered. Fear ye not therefore, ye are of more value than many sparrows.'"

"I think God was very good to give us our father and mother and grandma and brother Max, too, and our nice sisters, and—and all the rest of the folks," remarked Ned reflectively.

"I am very glad you appreciate all these great blessings, my little son," said his mother's voice close at his side.

"Yes, mamma. And oh, mamma! Can't Elsie and I go along with the rest of you when you go to New Orleans tomorrow?"

"I think so," she replied with a smile. "I am pretty sure your father will say yes if you ask him. Then he will have all his children along, and that is what he likes."

"He and Uncle Harold went down to see the servants," said Elsie. "Here they come now."

Ned hurried to meet them, preferred his request, and the next moment he came running back with the joyful announcement, "Papa says, 'yes, we may.' Oh, Elsie, aren't you glad?"

"Yes," she said. "I always like to be with papa and mamma and grandma, and it's ever so pleasant to be on our yacht."

"'Specially when we have both papa and brother Max to make it go all right," said Ned.

"You think it takes the two of us, do you?" laughed his father, taking a seat near his wife and drawing the little fellow in between his knees.

"No, papa. I know you could do it all by your own self," returned Ned. "But when brother Max is there, you don't have to take the trouble to mind how things are going all the time."

"No, that is certainly a fact," returned his father with a pleased laugh. "Brother Max can be trusted, and he knows how to manage that large vessel quite as well as his papa does. But what will you and little Elsie do while we older people are shopping?"

"Why, my dear, there will be so many of us that we will hardly all want to go at once," remarked Violet. "I think there will always be someone willing to stay with the little folks."

"Yes, mamma," said Gracie, who had drawn near, "I shall. Shopping is apt to tire me a good deal, and I think I shall prefer to spend the most of the time on the *Dolphin*."

"Yes, daughter, it may certainly be better for you," her father said, giving her an appreciative smile. "You can go when you wish and feel able and keep quiet and rest when you will. But we will leave the rest of our talk about the trip until tomorrow, choosing for the present some subject better suited to the sacredness of the day. I woud like to hear the verses that my children have ready to recite to me."

"Yes, sir," said Gracie. "Shall I go and tell Max and Lu that you are ready?"

"You may," the captain answered, and she went to return in a moment with her brother and sister, Chester and Eva.

"Why, I have quite a class," the captain said with a look of pleasure.

"I esteem it a privilege to be permitted to make one of the number, captain," said Chester.

"As we all do, I think," said Eva.

"Thank you both," said the captain. "Our subject today is grace—God's grace to us. Can you give me a verse that teaches it, Chester?"

"Yes, sir. Paul says in his epistle to the Ephesians, 'That in the ages to come He might shew exceeding riches of His grace, in His kindness toward us through Christ Jesus. For by grace are ye saved through faith; and that not of yourselves; it is the gift of God.'"

"'Being justified freely by His grace through the redemption that is in Christ Jesus,'" quoted Max in his turn.

Then Evelyn, "'Therefore it is of faith, that it might be by grace; to the end the promise might be sure to all the seed; not to that only which is of the law, but to that also which is of the faith of Abraham; who is the father of us all.'"

Lucilla's turn came next, and she repeated a verse from Second Peter, "'Grow in grace, and in the knowledge of our Lord and Savior Jesus Christ. To Him be glory both now and forever. Amen.'"

"I have two verses that seem to go well together," said Violet. "The first is in Proverbs, 'Surely He scorneth the scorners: but He giveth grace unto the lowly.' The other is in James, 'But He giveth more grace. Wherefore He saith, "God resisteth the proud but giveth grace unto the humble."'"

It was Gracie's turn, and she repeated with a look of joy, "'For the Lord God is a sun and shield; the Lord will give grace and glory; no good thing will He withhold from them that walk uprightly.

Oh, Lord of hosts, blessed is the man that trusteth in Thee.'"

"I have a little one, papa," said his daughter, Elsie. "'Looking diligently lest any man fail of the grace of God.'"

"This is mine, and it is short, too," said Ned. "'Thou therefore, my son, be strong in the grace that is in Christ Jesus.'"

"Yes, my boy, that is a short verse, but it is long enough if you will be careful to put it into practice," said his father.

Grandma Elsie, sitting near, had been listening attentively to the quotations of the younger people, and now she joined in with one, "'And of His fullness have all received, and grace for grace. For the law was given by Moses, but grace and truth came by Jesus Christ.' 'Wherefore gird up the loins of your mind, be sober, and hope to the end for the grace that is to be brought unto you at the revelation of Jesus Christ.'"

As she ceased, Cousin Ronald, who had drawn near, joined in the exercise, repeating the text, "'What shall we say then? Shall we continue in sin that grace may abound? . . . Shall we sin because we are not under the law, but under grace? God forbid.'" Then, at the captains request, Cousin Ronald followed them with a few pertinent remarks. A little familiar talk from the captain followed, and then came the call to the tea table. All retired early to their beds that night, so they might be ready to leave them early in the morning and set out in good season on their trip to the city. They succeeded in so doing, all feeling well and in the best of spirits.

The weather was fine, their voyage a prosperous one without any remarkable adventure, and the shopping proved quite as interesting and enjoyable as any of the shoppers had expected.

They all made the yacht their headquarters while they stayed, and the little ones hardly left it at all. They had always a companion—generally it was Gracie. As usual, she exerted herself for their entertainment, playing games with them and telling them stories or reading aloud from some interesting book.

All enjoyed the return voyage to Viamede and the warm welcome from Grandpa and Grandma Dinsmore upon their arrival there. Then it was a pleasure to display their purchases and hear the admiring comments upon them. The bridal veil and the material for the wedding dress were greatly admired, and all the purchases were highly approved of by both these grandparents and the relatives from the Parsonage, Magnolia, and Torriswood—all of whom came in early in the evening, full of interest in the results of the shopping expedition.

They had a pleasant social time together, the principal topic of conversation being the bride's trousseau and the various arrangements for the coming festivities to be had in connection with the approaching marriage.

Chester had been very generous in providing the trousseau, and Sydney was very grateful to him. Each of the Raymonds made her a gift of a handsome piece of silver, and Grandma Elsie added a beautiful set of jewelry. Sydney was delighted with her gifts. "Oh, Ches, but you are good to me!" she exclaimed with glad tears in her eyes. "And all the rest of you, dear friends and relatives, how can I thank you? This jewelry, Cousin Elsie, is lovely, and I shall always think of you when I wear it. All the silver is just beautiful, too, and indeed everything. I feel as rich as a queen."

"And when you have Cousin Bob added to all the rest, how do you suppose you are going to stand it?" laughed Harold.

"Oh, as the gifts are partly to him, he will help me to stand it," Sydney returned with a smiling glance at her affianced.

"I'll do my best," he answered, returning her smile with a broad one of his own.

"You simply must not allow yourselves to be overwhelmed yet," remarked Mr. Embury, "when not half the relatives and friends have been heard from as of yet."

"And I'll warrant my sister Betty will remember my bride with something worth while," remarked the bridegroom-elect.

"Yes, she will. I haven't a doubt of it," said Mrs. Embury. "And as they are in good circumstances, it will no doubt be something handsome."

"Of course, it will," said Dick. "Sister Betty was always a generous soul, taking delight in giving."

"Being related to you both, Bob and Syd, I want to give you something worthwhile. What would you like it to be?" said Mrs. Keith.

"Oh, never mind, Isa," exclaimed Dr. Johnson, jocosely. "Your husband is to tie the knot, and if he does it right—as no doubt he will—he will give me my bride. And that will be the best, the most valuable gift any one could bestow upon me."

"Yes," laughed Isa. "But it won't hurt you to have something else—something from me, too."

"Oh, by the way, why shouldn't we have a triple wedding?" exclaimed Maud. "I think it would be just lovely! It struck me so when I heard yesterday of the engagement of Max and Eva."

At that, the the four young people colored, the girls looking slightly embarrassed, but no one spoke for a moment or two.

"Don't you think it would make a very pretty wedding, Cousin Vi?" asked Maud.

"I dare say it would, Maud," replied Mrs. Raymond. "But our young folks are too young yet for marriage, my husband thinks, and should they all wait for a year or two. Besides," she added with playful look and tone, "there would be hardly time to make ready a proper trousseau for either, and certainly not for both."

"Oh, well, I hardly expected to be able to bring it about," returned Maud. "But I certainly do think it would be pretty."

"So it would," said Mrs. Embury, "very pretty, indeed. But that wouldn't pay for hurrying anyone into marriage before he or she is ready."

"No," said Cousin Ronald. "It is always best to make haste slowly in matters so vitally important."

"Wouldn't you be willing to make haste quickly in this instance, dearest?" queried Chester in a low aside to Lucilla—for, as usual, they sat near together.

"No," she returned with a saucy smile. "I find courting times too pleasant to be willing to cut them short—even if father would let me. And I know he would not."

"And he won't let the other couple either, which is good, since misery loves company."

"Ah, is courting me such hard work?" she asked, knitting her brows in pretended anger and disgust.

"Delightful work, but taking you for my very own would be still better."

"Ah, but you see that Captain Raymond stills considers me one of the little girls who are too young yet to leave their fathers."

"Well, you know I am pledged never to take you away from him."

"Yes, I am too happy in the knowledge of that ever to forget it. But do you know I for one should not fancy being married along with other couples—one ceremony serving for all of them. I should hardly feel sure the thing had been thoroughly and rightly done."

"Shouldn't you?" laughed Chester. "Well, then, we will certainly have the minister and ceremony all to ourselves whenever we do have it."

Just then, the lady visitors rose to take leave, and Chester, who had promised to return with Dr. and Mrs. Percival to Torriswood for the night, had time for but a few words with Lucilla. "I hope to be here again tomorrow pretty soon after breakfast," he said. "I grudge every hour spent away from your side, my dearest."

"Really, you flatter me," she laughed. "I doubt if anybody else appreciates my society so highly."

"You are probably mistaken as to that," he said. "I am quite aware that I am not your only admirer, and I feel highly flattered by your preference for me, Lu."

"Do you?" she laughed. "Well, I think it would not be prudent to tell you how great it is—if I could. Good night," giving him her hand, which he lifted to his lips.

As usual, she had a bit of chat with her father before retiring to her sleeping apartment for the night, and in that she repeated something of this little talk with Chester. "Yes, he is very much in love, and he finds it hard to wait," said the captain. "But I am no more ready to give up my daughter than he is to wait for her."

"I am in no hurry, papa," said Lucilla. "I do so love to be with you and under your care—and authority," she added with a mirthful, loving look up into his eyes.

"Yes, daughter dear, but do you expect to escape entirely from that last when you marry?"

"No, sir, and I don't want to. I really do love to be directed and controlled by you—my own father."

"I think no man ever had a dearer child than this one of mine," he said with emotion, drawing her into his arms and caressing her with great tenderness. He held her close for a moment and releasing her, bade her go and prepare for her night's rest.

Max and Evelyn were again sauntering along near the bayou, enjoying a bit of private chat before separating for the night.

"What do you think of Maud's proposition, Eva?" he asked.

"It seems hardly worthwhile to think about it at all, Max," she replied in a mirthful tone, "at least not if one cares for a trousseau or for pleasing your father in regard to the time of—you know, taking that important step of tying that knot that we cannot untie again should we grow ever so tired of it."

"I have no fear of that last so far as my feelings are concerned, dearest, and I hope you have none," he said in a tone that spoke some slight uneasiness.

"Not the slightest," she hastened to reply. "I think we know each other too thoroughly to indulge any such doubts and fears. Still, as I have great faith in your father's wisdom, and courting times are not by any means unpleasant, I feel in no haste to bring them to an end. You make such a delightful courter, Max, that the only thing I feel in a hurry about is the right to call the dear captain father."

"Ah, I don't wonder that you are in haste for that," returned Max. "I should be sorry indeed not to have that right. He is a father to love and to be proud of."

"He is indeed," she responded. "I fell in love with him at first sight, and I have loved him more and more ever since—for the better one knows him the more admirable and lovable he seems."

"I think that is true," said Max. "I am very proud of my father and earnestly desire to have him proud of me."

"Which he evidently is," returned Eva. "I don't wonder at it."

"Thank you," laughed Max. Then he added more gravely, "I hope I may never do anything to disgrace him."

"I am sure you never will," returned Eva in a tone that seemed to say such a thing could not be possible. "Had we not better retrace our steps to the house now?" she asked the next moment.

"Probably," said Max. "I presume father would say I ought not to deprive you of your beauty sleep. But these private walks and chats are so delightful to me, I am apt to be selfish about prolonging them."

"And your experience on board the ship has accustomed you to late hours, I suppose?"

"Yes, and to rather irregular times of sleeping and waking. A matter of small importance, however, when one gets used to it."

"But there would be the rub with me," she laughed, "in the getting used to it."

CHAPTER TWELFTH

"COUSIN RONALD, can't you make some fun for us?" asked Ned at the breakfast table the next morning. "We haven't had any of your kind since we came here."

"Well, and what of that, youngster? Must you live on fun all the time?" asked a rather rough voice directly behind the little boy.

"Oh! Who are you? And how did you come in here?" he asked, turning half round in his chair in an effort to see the speaker. "Oh, pshaw! You're nobody. Was it you, Cousin Ronald, or was it brother Max?"

"Polite little boys do not call gentlemen nobodies," remarked another voice that seemed to come from a distant corner of the room.

"And I didn't mean to," said Ned, "but the things I want to say will twist up, somehow."

"That bird you are eating looks good," said the same voice. "Couldn't you spare me a leg?"

"Oh, yes," laughed Ned. "If you'll come and get it. But one of these little legs wouldn't be much more than a bite for you."

"Well, a bite would be better than no breakfast at all, and somebody might give me one of those nice-looking rolls."

"I'm sure of it if you'll come to the table and show yourself," replied Ned.

"Here I am, then," said the voice close at his side.

"Oh, are you?" returned Ned. "Well, then, help yourself. You can have anything you choose to take, sir."

"Now, Ned, do you call that polite?" laughed Lucilla. "As you invite him to the table, you surely ought to help him to what he has asked for."

At that, Ned looked scrutinizingly at Cousin Ronald's plate, then at his brother's, and seeing that both were well filled, remarked, "I see he's well helped already and oughtn't to be asking for more till he gets that eaten up."

"Oh, you know too much, young man," laughed Max. "It isn't worth while for Cousin Ronald and me to waste our talents upon you."

"Oh, yes, it is, brother Max," said the little fellow. "It's fun, even though I do know it's one or the other or both of you."

"Oh, Cousin Ronald," exclaimed Elsie. "Can't you make some fun at the wedding, as you did when Cousin Betty was married? I don't remember much of it myself, but I've heard other folks tell about it."

"Why not ask Max instead of me, little dearie?" queried Mr. Lilburn.

"Oh!" cried the little girl. "I'd like to have both of you do it. It's much more fun with two than with only one."

"And it might be well to consult cousins Maud and Dick about it," suggested Grandma Elsie. "You can do so today, as we are all invited to take lunch at Torriswood."

"Are we? Oh, that's nice!" exclaimed little Elsie, smiling brightly. "You'll let us go, papa, won't you?"

"Yes. I expect to take you there."

"And if we all go, Cousin Ronald and Max might make some fun for us there. I guess the Torriswood folks would like it," remarked Ned insinuatingly.

"But might you not grow tired—having so much of it?" asked Max.

"No, indeed!" cried the little fellow. "It's too much fun for anybody to get tired of it."

"Any little chap like you, perhaps," remarked the strange voice from the distant corner.

"Pooh! I'm not so very little now," returned Ned.

"Not too little to talk a good deal," laughed Grandpa Dinsmore.

"This is a lovely morning," remarked Dr. Harold. "The roads are in fine condition, too, and I think the distance to Torriswood is not too great to make a very pleasant walk for those of us who are young and strong."

"And there are riding horses and conveyances in plenty for any who prefer to use them," added his mother hospitably.

Evelyn, Lucilla, and Max all expressed their desire to try the walk, and Gracie said, "I should like to try it, too." But both her father and Dr. Harold put a veto upon that, saying she was not strong enough, and that she must be content to ride.

"Cousin Ronald and brother Max, can't we have some fun there today, as well as at the wedding time?" asked Ned in his most coaxing tones.

"Possibly, bit laddie," returned the old gentleman pleasantly. "If I am no' too auld, your good brother is no' too young."

"But you are the more expert of the two, sir," said Max. "And perhaps it will be the better plan for us both to take part."

"Ah, well, we'll see when the time comes," responded the old gentleman. "I like well to please the bit laddie, if it can be done without vexing or disturbing anybody else."

"I don't think it can do that," observed Ned. "It's good fun, and everybody likes fun. Even my papa does," he added with a smiling glance up into his father's face.

"Yes, when it does not annoy or weary anyone else," the captain said in return.

"Will Chester be over this morning after breakfast, Lu?" asked Violet.

"He expected to when he went away last night," was the reply. "But he may not come if he hears that we are to go there."

"I think he is too much a man of his word to be hindered by that," her father said, giving her a reassuring smile.

And he was right, for Chester was with them even a little earlier than usual.

"Maud told me you were all coming over to lunch with her," he said. "But as some of you have never seen the place, I thought you might not object to a pilot, and the exercise would be rather beneficial to me."

"You are quite right there," said Harold. "You know that as your physician, I have prescribed a good deal of outdoor exercise."

"Yes. I have been taking the prescription, too, and I find it beneficial, especially when I am so fortunate as to secure pleasant company." His glance at Lucilla as he spoke seemed to imply that there was none more desirable than hers.

"Then, as the walk is a long one, I would suggest that we start as soon as may suit the convenience of the ladies," said Harold. Both Evelyn and Lucilla hastened to make such preparation as they deemed necessary or desirable.

The Parsonage was scarcely a stone's throw out of their path, and they called there on their way. They owed Isadore a call and were willing to make one upon her sister Virginia also—now making her home at the Parsonage—though she had not as yet called upon them.

They found both ladies upon the veranda. Isadore gave them a joyful welcome, Virginia a cool one, saying, "I should have called upon you before now, but I know poor relations are not apt to prove welcome visitors."

"But I thought you were making your home at Viamede," said Dr. Harold.

"No, not since Dick and Bob removed to Torriswood. I couldn't think of living on there alone. So I came here to Isa, she being my nearest of kin in this part of the world."

Harold thought he did not envy Isa on that account, but he quite prudently refrained from saying so.

Isa invited them to stay and spend the day there, but they declined, stating that they were on their way to Torriswood by invitation.

"Yes," said Virginia. "Of course, they can invite rich relations but entirely neglect poor me."

"Why, Virgie," exclaimed Isadore in surprise, "I am sure you have been invited there more than once since you have been here."

"Well, I knew it was only a duty invitation, and they didn't really want me. So I didn't go. I have a little more sense than to impose my company upon people who don't really want it."

"I shouldn't think anybody would while you show such an ugly temper," thought Lucilla, but she refrained from saying it. She and her companions made but a short call, presently bade good-bye, and continued on their way to Torriswood.

They received a warm welcome there and were presently joined by the rest of their party from Viamede. There was some lively and animated chat in regard to letters sent and letters received, the making of the wedding dress, and various other preparations for the coming ceremony, to all of which little Ned listened rather impatiently. Then, as soon as a pause in the conversation gave him an opportunity, he turned to Dr. Percival, saying, "Cousin Dick, wouldn't it be right nice to have a little fun?"

"Fun, Neddie? Why, certainly, my boy. Fun is often quite beneficial to the health. But how shall we manage it? Have you a good joke for us?"

"No, sir," said Ned. "But you know we have two ventriloquists here, and — and I like the kind of fun they make. Don't you?"

"It is certainly very amusing sometimes, and I see no objection if our friends are willing to favor us with some specimens of their skill," was the reply, accompanying a glance first at Mr. Lilburn and then at Max.

"Oh!" exclaimed Maud. "That might be a good entertainment for our wedding guests!"

"Probably," returned her husband, "but if it is to be used then it would be well not to let our servants into the secret beforehand."

"Decidedly so, I should say," said Max. "It would be far better to reserve that entertainment for that time."

"But surely it would do no harm to give us a few examples of your skill today, when the servants are out of the room," said Maud.

"No, certainly not, if anything worth while could be thought of," said Max. "But it seems to me that it must be quite an old story with all of us here."

"Not to me, brother Max," exclaimed Ned. "And the funny things you and Cousin Ronald seem to make invisible folks say make other people laugh as well as me."

"And laughter is helpful to digestion," said a strange voice, apparently speaking from the doorway. "But should folks digest too well these doctors might find very little to do. So it is not to be wondered at if they object greatly to letting much fun be made."

"But the doctor's haven't objected," laughed Dr. Percival. "And I have no fear that work from them will fail even if some of their patients should laugh and grow fat."

"I presume that's what the little fellow that wants the fun has been doing," said the voice. "For in regard to fat, he is prime condition."

At that Ned colored and looked slightly vexed. "Papa, am I so very fat?" he asked.

"None too fat to suit my taste, my son," replied the captain, smiling kindly on the little fellow.

"And you certainly wouldn't want to be nothing but a little bag of bones, would you?" queried the voice.

"No," returned Ned sturdily. "I'd a great deal rather be fat. Bones are ugly things anyway."

"Good to cover up with fat, but they are quite necessary underneath it," said the voice. "You couldn't stand or walk if you had no bones."

"No, to be sure not. Though I never thought about it before," returned Ned. "Some ugly things are worth more, after all, than some pretty ones."

"Very true," said the voice. "So we must not despise anything merely because it lacks beauty."

"Is it you talking, Cousin Ronald, or is it brother Max?" asked Ned, looking searchingly first at one and then at the other.

"No matter which, laddie," said the gentleman. "And who shall say it hasn't been both of us?"

"Oh, yes, maybe it was! I couldn't tell at all," exclaimed Ned.

Lunch was now ready, and all repaired to the table. The blessing had been asked, and all were sitting quietly as Dr. Percival took up a knife to carve the fowl. "Don't, oh, don't!" seemed to come from it in a terrified scream. "I'm all right. No need of a surgeon's knife."

Everyone was startled for an instant, the doctor nearly dropping his knife. Then there was a general laugh, and the carving proceeded without further objection. The servants were all out the room at the moment.

"Ah, Cousin Ronald, that reminds me of very old times, when I was a little child," said Violet, giving the old gentleman a mirthful look.

"Ah, yes!" he said. "I remember now that I was near depriving you of your share of the fowl when breakfasting one morning at your father's hospitable board. Have you not yet forgiven that act of indiscretion, my dear?"

"Indeed, yes, fully and freely long ago. But it was really nothing to forgive—your intention having been to afford amusement to us all."

"Neddie, shall I help you? Are you willing to eat a fowl that can scream out so much like a human creature?" asked Dr. Percival.

"Oh, yes, Cousin Doctor, 'cause I know just how he did it," laughed the little boy.

Then the talk about the table turned upon the various matters connected with the subject of the approaching wedding—whether this or that relative would be likely to come for the wedding; when he or she might be expected to arrive, and where be entertained; the adornment of the grounds for the occasion; the fashion in which each of the bride's new dresses should be made and what jewelry, if any, she should wear when dressed for the ceremony; and also about a maid of honor and bridesmaids.

"I want to have two or three little flower girls," said Sydney. "I have thought of Elsie Dinsmore, Elsie Embury, and Elsie Raymond as the ones I should prefer. They are near enough of an age, all related to me, and all quite pretty—at least they will look so when handsomely dressed," she added with a laughing look at the one present, who blushed and seemed slightly embarrassed for a moment. But she said not a word.

"I highly approve if we can get the other two here in season," said Maud.

"For my maid of honor, I must have one of you older girls," continued Sydney. "Perhaps I'll want all three. I don't know yet how many groomsmen Robert is going to have."

"Cousin Harold and my friend Max, if they will serve," said Robert, glancing inquiringly at them in turn.

"Thank you, Bob," said Harold. "Seeing you are a brother physician—cousin as well—I cannot think of refusing. In fact I consider myself quite honored."

Max also accepted the invitation with suitable words, and the talk went on.

"Are you expecting to take a trip?" asked Harold.

"Yes, we talk of going to the Bahamas," said Robert. "It is said to be a delightful winter resort, and neither of us has ever been there."

"Then I think you will be likely to enjoy your visit there greatly," responded Harold.

"So we think," said Robert. "But now about groomsmen. I'd also like to add your brother Herbert and Sydney's brother, Frank, if we can get them here, and they are willing to serve. Chester won't, because Lu must not be a bridesmaid, having served twice already in that capacity. And you know the old saying, 'Three times a bridesmaid, never a bride.'"

"I have little doubt of the willingness of the lads if they are here in season," returned Harold. "But I think Herbert's movements will depend largely upon those of Cousin Arthur. It would hardly do for all three of us to absent ourselves from professional duties at the same time."

"But Frank can be spared from his, I suppose?" Robert said inquiringly, turning to Chester as he spoke the question.

"Yes, for a short time, I think," was Chester's prompt reply.

"Come, let us all go out on the lawn and consult in regard to the best place for having the arch made under which our bridal party are to stand," Maud said, addressing the company in general as they left the table. The invitation was accepted, and they spent some time in strolling about under the trees, chatting familiarly. The principal topic was the one proposed by Mrs. Percival, but they also considered the question where it would be best to set the tables for the wedding guests.

"It is likely to be a large company," said Maud. "But I think we can accommodate them all quite comfortably here."

"Yes. I should think so," said Grandma Elsie. "Your lawn is large and lovely. I am very glad, Dick, that you secured so beautiful a place."

"Thank you, cousin," he returned. "I think I was fortunate in getting it, as Maud does, too. She likes it quite well."

"And you prefer it to Viamede?"

"Only because it is my own," he answered with a smile. "One could not find a lovelier place than Viamede anywhere on earth."

"But you lost the housekeeping of your cousin Virginia by making the change," Harold observed with a humorous look.

"Hardly!" laughed Dick. "She was that but in name. And the change to Isa's housekeeping and companionship must be rather agreeable to her, I should think."

"She seems to me much the more agreeable of the two," said Harold.

"Yes. Isa is a lovely woman, and Virginia has her good qualities, too."

As Torriswood was but little farther from the bayou than Viamede, it was presently decided by the young people that they would return by boat. Upon starting, they found it so pleasant that they took a much longer sail, reaching their destination barely in time for tea.

"Does Sydney's evident happiness in the near approach of her marriage make my little girl unhappy and discontented with her father's decision in regard to hers?" asked Captain Raymond, when Lucilla came to him for the usual bit of good night chat.

"Oh, no, papa. No, indeed!" she exclaimed with a low, happy laugh. "Have you forgotten, or don't you know yet, how dearly that same little girl loves to be with you?"

"Really, I believe she does," he said, caressing her with tenderness. "And though it is undeniably partly for his own—her father's—sake, that he insists upon delay, it is still more for yours. I do believe that you are yet much too young for the cares and duties of married life. I want you to have a good play-day before going into them," he added with another caress.

"You dear, kind father!" she said in response. "I could wish to be always a child if so I might be always with you."

"Well, daughter, we may hope for many more years together in this world and a blessed eternity together in heaven."

"Yes, papa, there is great happiness in that thought. Oh, I am glad and thankful that God gave me a Christian father."

"And I that I have every reason to believe that my dear, eldest daughter has learned to know and love Him. To belong to Christ is better than to have the wealth of the world. Riches take to themselves wings and fly away, but He has said, 'I will never leave thee, nor forsake thee.'"

"Such a sweet, precious promise, father!"

"Yes. It may well relieve us from care and anxiety about the future, especially as taken in connection with that other promise, 'As thy days, so shall thy strength be.'"

"Don't you think, papa, that if we remember and fully believe the promises of God's word we might—or better said—we should be happy under all circumstances?"

"I do indeed Lulu," he said emphatically. "We all need to pray as the disciples did, 'Lord increase our faith,' for 'without faith it is impossible to please Him.'"

CHAPTER THIRTEENTH

THE NEXT THREE WEEKS passed delightfully to the friends at Viamede. There were drives, boating, and fishing excursions, not to speak of rambles through the woods and fields and quiet home pleasures. The approaching wedding and the preparations for it greatly interested them all, especially the young girls. It was pleasantly exciting to watch the making of the bride's dresses and of their own intended to be worn on that important occasion. Besides, after a little while there were various arrivals of relations and friends to whom invitations had been sent—the whole families from Riverside, Ion, Fairview, the Oaks, the Laurels, Beechwood, and Roselands.

Herbert Travilla would have denied himself the pleasure of the trip in order that Dr. Arthur Conly might take a much-needed rest, but it was finally decided that both might venture to absent themselves from their practice for a short season.

All Grandma Elsie's children and grandchildren were taken in at Viamede, making the house very full. The rest were accommodated with the other relatives at the Parsonage, Magnolia Hall, and Torriswood—in which last-named place the family from the Oaks were domiciled. It was not until a few days before that appointed for the wedding that the last of the relatives from a distance arrived.

To the extreme satisfaction of all concerned, the wedding day dawned bright and beautiful—not a cloud in the sky. The ceremony was to be at noon, and the guests came pouring in shortly before the appointed hour.

The grounds were looking their loveliest—the grass like emerald velvet bespangled with fragrant flowers of every hue. The trees were laden with foliage, and some of them—the oranges and magnolias in particular—bore blossoms. Under these an arch, covered with smilax, had been erected, and from its center hung a large bell formed of the lovely and fragrant orange blossoms. The clapper was made of crimson roses. Under that, the bridal party presently took their stand.

First came the three little flower girls—Elsie Dinsmore, Elsie Raymond, and Elsie Embury—dressed in white silk mull. Each carried a basket of white roses. The bridesmaids and groomsmen followed—Frank Dinsmore with Corinne Embury, Harold Travilla with Gracie Raymond, Herbert Travilla and Mary Embury. The girls were all dressed in white and carried bouquets of smilax and white flowers.

Max had declined to serve on hearing that Eva could not serve with him on account of being still in mourning for her mother.

Lastly came the bride and groom, Sydney looking very charming in a white silk trimmed with an abundance of costly lace, wearing a beautiful bridal veil and wreath of fragrant orange blossoms, and carrying a bouquet of the same in her hand.

The party stood beneath the arch, the bride and groom directly beneath the bell in its center, while the guests gathered about them, the nearest relatives taking the nearest stations.

Mr. Cyril Keith was the officiating minister. It was a pretty ceremony, but short, and then the congratulations and good wishes began.

Those rituals over, the guests were invited to seat themselves about a number of tables scattered here and there under the trees and loaded with tempting viands. The minister asked a blessing upon the food, and the feast began.

An effort had been made to some extent to seat the guests so that relatives and friends would be near each other. The entire bridal party was at one table, and the other young people of the connection were pretty close at hand. The older ones and their children not much farther off.

Everybody had been helped to their food, and cheery chat, mingled with some mirth, was going on, when suddenly a shrill voice, that seemed to come from the branches overhead, cried out, "What you 'bout, all you folks? Polly wants some breakfast."

Everybody started and looked up into the tree from which the sounds had seemed to come, but no parrot was visible there.

"Why, where is the bird?" asked several voices in tones of surprise. But hardly had the question been asked when another parrot seemed to speak from a table near that at which the bridal party sat. "Polly's hungry. Poor, old Polly—poor, old soul!"

"Is that so, Polly? Then just help yourself," said Dr. Percival.

"Polly wants her coffee. Poor, old Polly, poor, old soul!" came in reply, sounding as if the bird had gone farther down the table.

Then a whistle was heard that seemed to come from some distance among the trees, and hardly had it ceased when there was a loud call, "Come on, my merry men, and let us get our share of this grand wedding feast."

"Tramps about! And bold ones they must be!" exclaimed one of the neighborhood guests.

"Really, I hope they are not going to make any trouble!" cried another. "I fear we have no weapons of defense among us, and if we had I for one would be loath to turn a wedding feast into a fight."

"Hark! Hark!" cried another, as the notes of a bugle came floating on the breeze, the next minute accompanied by what seemed to be the sound of a drum and a fife playing a national air. "What, what can it mean? I have heard of no troops in this neighborhood. But that's martial music, and now," as another sound met the ear, "don't you hear the tramp, tramp?"

"Yes, yes, it certainly must be troops. But who or what can have called them out?" asked a fourth guest, starting to his feet as if contemplating rushing away to try to catch a glimpse of the quickly approaching soldiers.

"Oh, sit down and let us go on with our wedding breakfast," expostulated still another. "Of course, they are American troops on some trifling errand in the neighborhood and not going to interfere with us. There! The music has stopped, and I don't hear their tramp either. Dr. Percival," turning in his host's direction and raising his voice, "can you account for that martial music playing a moment since?"

"I haven't heard of any troops about, but I am quite sure they will not interfere with us," returned the doctor. "Please, friends, don't let it disturb you at all." Little Ned Raymond was looking on and listening in an ecstasy of delight.

"Oh, Cousin Ronald and brother Max, do some more!" he entreated in a subdued but urgent tone. "Folks do believe it's real soldiers, and it's such fun to see how they look and talk about it."

The martial music and the tramp, tramp began again and seemed to draw nearer and nearer. Several dogs belonging on the place rushed away in that direction, barking furiously.

It seemed to excite and disturb many of the guests, and Violet said, "There, my little son, I think that ought to satisfy you for the present. Let our gentlemen and everybody else here have their breakfast in peace."

"Good advice, Cousin Vi," said Mr. Lilburn. "The wee bit of a laddie may get his fill of such fun at another time."

"Really, I don't understand it at all," remarked a lady seated at the same table with the gentleman who had called to Dr. Percival. "That martial music has ceased with great suddenness, and I no longer hear the tramp, tramp of the troops."

"I begin to have a very strong suspicion that ventriloquism is responsible for it all," returned the gentleman with a smile. "Did you not hear at the time of the marriage of Dr. Johnson's sister that a ventriloquist was present and made a rare sport of the guests?"

"Oh, yes, I think I did and that he was one of the relatives. I presume he is here now and responsible for these strange sounds. But," she added thoughtfully, "there are several sounds going on at once. Could he make them all, do you think?"

"Perhaps the talent runs in the family, and there is more than one here possessing it."

"Ah, yes, that must be it," remarked another guest, nodding wisely. "I presume it must run in the family. What sport it must make for them."

"But what has become of those tramps—the merry men who were going to claim a share of this feast?" queried a young girl seated at the same table.

"Perhaps they have joined the troops," laughed another. "But hark! They are at it again," as a shrill whistle once more came floating on the breeze from the same direction as before, followed by the words, "Come on, my merry men. Let us make haste ere all the best of the viands have disappeared down the throats of the fellows already there."

Mr. Hugh Lilburn had overheard the chat about the neighboring table and thought best to gratify the desire to hear further from the merry men of the wood.

A good many eyes were turned in the direction of the sounds, but none could see even one of the merry men so loudly summoned to make a raid upon the feasting company.

Then another voice seemed to reply from the same quarter as the first.

"The days of Robin Hood and his merry men are over lange syne, and this is no' the country for ony sic doin's. If we want a share o' the grand feast we maun ask it like decent, honest folk, tendering payment if that wad no' be considered an insult by the host an' hostess."

At that Dr. Percival laughed and called out in a tone of amusement, "Come on, friends, and let me help you to a share of the eatables. We have enough and to spare, and you will be heartily welcome."

"Many thanks, sir," said the voice. "Perhaps we may accept when your invited guests have eaten their fill and departed."

"Very well. Manage it to suit yourselves," laughed the doctor.

Then another voice from the wood said, "Well, comrades, let us sit down here under the trees and wait for our turn."

All this had caused quite an excitement and a great buzz of talk among the comparatively stranger guests. Yet they seemed to enjoy the dainty fare provided and ate heartily of it as they talked, listening, too, for a renewal of the efforts of the ventriloquists of the gathering.

But the latter refrained from any further exercise of their skill, as the time was drawing near when the bride and groom were to set out on their bridal trip. They and their principal attendants repaired to the house, where the bride exchanged her wedding gown for a very pretty and becoming traveling dress, her bridesmaids and intimate girls friends assisting her. Her dressing finished, they all ran down into the lower hall—already almost crowded with other guests. Laughing and excited, they all stood waiting her appearance at the head of the stairway. She was there in a moment—her bouquet of orange blossoms in her hand.

The hands of the party of laughing young girls were instantly extended toward her, and she threw the bouquet, saying merrily, "Catch it who can, and you will be the first to follow me into wedded happiness."

It so happened that Evelyn Leland and Lucilla Raymond stood so near together that their hands almost touched and that the bouquet fell to both—each catching it with one hand. Their success was hailed by a peal of laughter from all present, Chester Dinsmore and Max Raymond particularly seeming to enjoy the sport.

The bride came tripping down the stairway, closely followed by her groom, and the adieus began—not especially sad ones, as so many of the near and dear relatives left behind expected to see them again ere many weeks should pass. Quite a goodly number of the party followed them down to the edge of the bayou, where lay the boat that was to carry them over the first part of their wedding journey. They stepped aboard amid showers of rice accompanied by an old shoe or two, merry laughter, and many good wishes for a happy and prosperous trip. As they seated themselves, a beautiful horseshoe formed of lovely orange blossoms fell into the bride's lap.

The little vessel was bountifully adorned with flags of various sizes by the previous arrangement of Dr. Percival, who knew them both to be devoted admirers of the flag of the Union. As the vessel moved away, there came from among the trees at a little distance the sound of a bugle, the drum, and the fife playing the *Star-spangled Banner*. Nothing could have been more appropriate.

As the boat disappeared and the music died away, something of a lonely feeling came over many of those left behind, and the guests not related began to make their adieus and depart to their homes. But the relatives tarried somewhat longer, chatting familiarly among themselves and examining the many handsome bridal gifts.

"They have fared well," said Mrs. Betty Norton, Robert's sister. "I am so glad for them both. I'm fond of my brother and well pleased with the match he has made. And not less so with Dick's," she added, turning with a smile to Maud, who stood at her side.

"Thank you, Betty," said Maud. "I was well pleased with the relationship we held to each other before, and I am glad it has been made nearer. Though, at first, when Dick proposed, I was afraid it—the relationship—ought to be a bar to our union. However, he said it was not near enough for that, and as he is a good physician, I supposed he knew. So I did not say nay to him," she added with a laughing look up into her husband's face, as at that moment he drew near and stood at her side.

"Ah, don't you wish you had?" he returned, laying a hand lightly on her shoulder and giving her a very lover-like look and smile.

"I have objections to being questioned so closely," she said laughingly. "Remember, sir, that I did not promise never to have a secret from you even if you're my other—and perhaps—my better half."

"Oh, I always understood it was the woman's privilege to be that," he laughed. "I certainly expect it of you, my dear."

"Why, how absurd of you, darling!" she exclaimed. "With such a husband as mine, it would be utterly impossible for me to be the better half."

"But it is quite the thing for each to think the other is," said Grandma Elsie, regarding them with an affectionate smile.

"A state of feeling that is certain to make both very happy," remarked Captain Raymond, who happened to be standing near.

"As you and I know by experience," said Violet with a bright look up into his face.

"Yes," said her cousin, Betty. "And anybody who knows you two as well as I do may see the exemplification of that doctrine in your lives. I have always known that you were a decidedly happy couple."

"But you needn't plume yourself very much for that discovery, Cousin Betty," laughed Lucilla. "I think everybody makes it who is with them for even a day or two."

"And his children are not much, if at all, behind his wife in love for him or behind him in love for her," added Gracie, smiling up into her father's pleasant face.

"All doing their best to fill him with conceit," he said, returning the smile but with a warning shake of the head. "Where are Elsie and Ned?" he asked, adding, "It is about time we were returning home—to Viamede."

"Yes," said Violet. "We must hunt the two of them up at once."

"I will find them, papa and mamma," Gracie answered, hastening from the room.

The children were playing games on the lawn, but all ceased and came running to Gracie as she stepped out upon the veranda and called in musical tones to her little sister and brother.

"What is it?" they asked as they drew near. "Is it time to go home?"

"Yes, so papa and mamma think, and we must always do what they say, you know."

"Yes, indeed!" answered Elsie. "And it's just a pleasure because they always know best and are so kind and love us so dearly."

"We've been having an elegant time, and it's just lovely here at Torriswood," said little Elsie Embury. "But as it is Uncle Dick's place, we can come here often. Besides, Viamede is quite as pretty, and we are to go there for the rest of the day."

"Oh, yes! Aren't you glad?" responded several other young voices.

The carriages that had brought them were now seen to be ready to convey them to that desired destination, and presently one after another received its quota and departed.

One three-seated vehicle contained Mrs. Travilla, her father and his wife, Captain and Mrs. Raymond, and their little girl and boy. Naturally, the talk ran upon the scenes through which they had just been passing.

"It was quite odd that Eva and Lu should have caught that bridal bouquet together," laughed Violet. "My dear, does it not make you tremble with apprehension lest those two weddings should take place somewhat sooner than you wish?"

"I cannot say that I am greatly alarmed," Captain Raymond returned pleasantly. "I have far too much confidence in the affection and desire to please their father of both my eldest son and daughter to greatly fear that they will disregard my wishes and opinion in reference to that, or anything else, for that matter."

"And I feel very sure that your confidence is not misplaced," said Mrs. Travilla. "Also I think you are wise in wishing them—young as they are—to defer marriage for a few years."

Mr. and Mrs. Dinsmore expressed a very hearty agreement in that opinion, and Violet said it was hers also. "But I could see," she added with a playful look and tone, "that the lovers were both pleased and elated. However, it is not supposed to mean speedy matrimony, but merely that they will be the first of those engaged in the sport to enter into it."

"Yes," Captain Raymond said laughingly, "and I know of one case in which the successful catcher—though the first of the competitors to enter into the bonds of matrimony—did not do so until six years afterward. So, naturally, I am not greatly alarmed."

A smaller vehicle, driving at some little distance in their rear, held the two young couples of whom they were speaking. With them also the episode of the throwing and catching of the bouquet was the subject of conversation.

"It was capitally done, girls," laughed Max. "It may even possibly encourage father to shorten our probation—somewhat at least."

"Yes, I am sure I wish it may," said Chester. "I hope you will not object, Lu?"

"I do not believe it would make a particle of difference in the result whether I did or not," she laughed. "If you knew father as well as I do, you would know that he does not often retreat from a position that he has once taken. And he is not superstitious enough to pay any attention to such an omen as we have had today. Nor would I wish him to, as I have the greatest confidence in his wisdom and his love for his children."

"To all of which I add an unqualified assent," said Max heartily. "My father's opinion on almost any subject has far more weight with me than that of any other man."

CHAPTER
FOURTEENTH

VIAMEDE PRESENTLY SHOWED as beautiful and festive a scene as had Torriswood earlier in the day—the velvety grass bespangled with sweet-scented flowers of varied hues, the giant oaks and magnolias, and the orange trees with their beautiful glossy leaves, green fruit and ripe, and lovely blossoms. Many flags floated here and there from upper windows, verandas, and tree tops. There were not a few exclamations of admiration and delight from the young people and children as carriage after carriage drove up and deposited its living cargo.

A very merry and mirthful time followed. Sports begun at Torriswood were renewed here with as much zest and spirit as had been shown there, the large company scattering about the extensive grounds and forming groups engaged in one or another game suited to the ages and capacity of its members. Some preferred strolling here and there through the alleys and groves, engaging in nothing more exciting or wearying than sprightly chat and laughter, while the older ladies and gentlemen— among them Mr. and Mrs. Dinsmore, Mr. and

Mrs. Ronald Lilburn, Mr. and Mrs. Hugh Lilburn, Mr. and Mrs. Embury, Rev. and Mrs. Keith, Mrs. Travilla, Mr. and Mrs. Leland, and Dr. Arthur Conley and his Marian—gathered in groups on the verandas or the nearer parts of the lawn.

Edward Travilla and Zoe were down among the little folks, overseeing the sports of their own twin boy and girl and their mates, as were also Captain Raymond and his Violet with their Elsie and Ned. His older son and daughters together with Chester Dinsmore, his brother Frank, and Evelyn Leland could be seen at some little distance, occupying rustic seats under a wide-spreading tree and seemingly enjoying an animated and amusing chat. Drs. Harold and Herbert Travilla, strolling along with the two older daughters of Mr. Embury, presently joined them, and Dr. and Mrs. Percival shortly followed, the mirth and jollity apparently increasing with each addition.

"They seem to be very merry over yonder," remarked Mrs. Embury with a smiling glance at that particular group. "It does me good to see Dick take a little relaxation. He is usually so busy in the practice of his profession."

"Yes," said Grandma Elsie. "The evidently strong affection between him and Maud is very delightful to see."

"As is that between the captain and Violet," added her cousin Annis. "I thought her young for him when they married, but I never saw a more attached couple. They make no display of it before people, but no close observer could be with them long without becoming convinced of the fact."

"That is so, I think," said Mrs. Leland. "Captain Raymond is a fond father, but he has told Vi more than once that to lose her would be worse to him than being called to part with all of his children."

"Ah, I hope neither trial may ever be appointed him," said Grandma Elsie, low and softly, ending with a slight sigh.

"So Chester and Lucilla, Max and Eva are engaged," remarked Mrs. Embury in a reflective tone. "And so far, the entire connection seems satisfied with the arrangement."

"I have yet to hear any kind of objection from any quarter," Mrs. Leland said with a smile. "I can say with certainty that Lester and I are well satisfied, so far as our niece Eva is concerned. I think the captain is right and wise though in bidding them delay marriage for at least a year or two—all of them being so young."

"I think," said Mrs. Arthur Conly, joining in the talk, "that Frank Dinsmore is evidently very much in love with Gracie."

"I sincerely hope he will get no encouragement from the captain," Dr. Conly added quickly and with strong emphasis. "Gracie is much too young, and she entirely too feeble to safely venture into wedlock for years to come."

"I think you may very safely trust her father to see that she does not," said Grandma Elsie. "I am sure he agrees in your opinion, and I am also sure that Gracie is too good and obedient a daughter ever to go contrary to his wishes."

Gradually, as the sun finally drew near his setting, the participants in the sports gave them up and gathered in the parlors or upon the verandas—most of them just about weary enough with the pleasant exercise they had been taking to enjoy a little quiet rest before being summoned to partake of the grand dinner in the process of preparation by Viamede's famous cooks.

Lucilla and her sister Gracie, wishing to make some slight change in the arrangement of hair and dress, hastened up the broad stairway together on their way to the room now occupied by Gracie and Elsie. In the upper hall they met their father, coming from a similar errand to his own apartment.

"Ah, daughters," he said in his usual kindly tones, "we have had much less than usual to say to each other today, but I hope you have been enjoying yourselves?" As he spoke, he put an arm around each and drew them closer to him.

"Oh, yes. Yes, indeed, papa!" both replied together, smilingly and in mirthful tones.

Lucilla added, "Everything seems to have gone beautifully. Don't you think, papa?"

"Even to the catching of the bride's bouquet, I suppose," returned her father, giving her an amused yet searching and half-inquiring look.

At that Lucilla laughed.

"Yes, papa. Wasn't it very odd that Eva and I happened to catch it together?"

"And were you both highly elated over the happy augury?" he queried, still gazing searchingly into her dark eyes.

"Hardly, I think, papa. Though Chester and Max seemed rather elated by it. But really," she added with a mirthful look, "I depend far more upon my father's decision than upon dozens of such auguries. Besides, I am in no haste to leave his care and protection or go from under his authority."

"Spoken like my own dear, eldest daughter," he returned with a gratified look, giving her a caress.

"It would be strange, indeed, if any one of your children did want to get from under it, papa," said Gracie with a look of ardent affection up into his eyes.

"I am glad to hear you say that, daughter," he returned with a smile, softly smoothing the shining, golden hair. "Because it will be years before I can be willing to resign the care of my still rather feeble little Gracie to another or let her take up the burdens and anxieties of married life."

"You may be perfectly sure I don't want to, papa," she returned with a gleeful, happy laugh. "It is just a joy and delight to me to feel that I belong to you and always shall as long as you want to keep me."

"Which will be just as long as you enjoy it—and we both live," he added a little more gravely.

Then releasing them with an injunction not to waste too much time over their preparations, he passed on down the stairway while they went on into their tiring-room.

"Oh, Lu," said Gracie, as she pulled down her hair before the glass, "haven't we the best and dearest father in the world? I like Chester ever so much, but I sometimes wonder how you can bear the very thought of leaving papa for him."

"It does not seem an easy thing to do," sighed Lucilla, "and yet—" But she paused, leaving her sentence unfinished.

"Yet, what?" asked Gracie, turning an inquiring look upon her sister.

"Well, I believe I'll tell you," returned Lucilla in a half-hesitating way. "I have always valued father's love oh, so highly. Once when I happened accidentally to overhear something he said to Mamma Vi, it nearly broke my heart—for a while anyway." Her voice quivered with the last words, and she seemed unable to go on for emotion.

"Why, Lu, what could it have been?" exclaimed Gracie in surprise, giving her sister a sweet look of mingled love and compassion.

With an evident effort, Lucilla went on, "It was that she was dearer to him than all his children put together—that he would lose every one of them rather than part with her. It made me feel for a while as if I had lost everything worth having—papa's love for me must be so very slight. But after a long and bitter cry over it, I was comforted by remembering what the Bible says, 'Let every one of you in particular so love his wife even as himself.' And the words of Jesus, 'For this cause shall a man leave father and mother, and cleave to his wife: and they twain shall be one flesh.' So I could see it was right for my father to love his wife best of all earthly creatures—she being but a part of himself—and besides I could not doubt that he loved me and each one of his children very, very dearly."

"Yes, I am sure he does," said Gracie, vainly trying to speak in her usual cheery, light-hearted tones. "Oh, Lu, I don't wonder you cried over it. It would just kill me to think papa didn't care very much about me."

"Oh, Gracie, he does! I know he does! I am sure he would not hesitate a moment to risk his life for any one of us."

"Yes, I am sure of it! And what but his love for you makes him so unwilling to give you up to Chester? I can see that Ches feels it hard to wait, but father certainly has the best rights to keep his daughters to himself so long as they are under age."

"And as much longer as he chooses, so far as I am concerned. I am only too glad that he seems so loath to give me up. My dear, dear father! Words cannot express my love for him or the regret I feel for the rebellious conduct that gave him so much pain and trouble in days long gone by."

"Dear Lu," said Gracie, "I am perfectly sure our dear father forgave all that long ago."

"Yes, but I can never forget or forgive it myself. Nor can I forget how glad and thankful he was that I was not the one killed by the bear out at Minersville, or his saving me that time when I was so nearly swept into Lake Erie by the wind. How closely he hugged me to himself—a tear falling on my head—when he got me safely into the cabin, and the low-breathed words, 'Thank God, my darling, precious child is safe in my arms.' Oh, Gracie, I have seemed to hear the very words and tones many a time since. So I cannot doubt that he does love me very much—even if I am not so dear to him as his wife is."

"And you love mamma, too?"

"Yes, indeed! She is just like a dear, older sister. I may love her since she is so dear to papa, and she was so kind and forbearing with me in those early years of her married life when I certainly was very far from being the good and lovable child I ought to have been. She was very forbearing, and she never gave papa the slightest hint of my badness."

"She has always been very good and kind to us," said Gracie. "I love her very dearly."

"And papa showed his love for me in allowing Chester to offer himself because he had saved my life—for otherwise he would have forbidden it for at least another year or two."

"Yes, I know," said Gracie. "We certainly have plenty of proofs that father does love us both very, very much."

"But we must not delay at this business, as he bade us hasten down again," Lucilla said, quickening her movements as she spoke.

"No. I'm afraid he will already be wondering what is keeping us so long," said Gracie, following her example.

But they had no idea how their father was engaged at that moment. As he reached the lower hall, Frank Dinsmore stepped forward and accosted him. "Can I have a moment's chat with you, captain?" he asked in an undertone and with a slightly embarrassed air.

"Certainly, Frank. It is a very modest request," was the kindly-toned response, "What can I do for you, young sir?"

"Very nearly the same thing that you have so kindly done for my brother, sir," replied the young man, coloring and hesitating somewhat in his speech. "I—I am deeply, desperately in love with your daughter, Miss Gracie, and—"

"Go no farther, my young friend," interrupted the captain in a grave, though still kindly tone. "I have no objections to you personally, but Gracie is entirely too young and too delicate for her father to consider for a moment the idea of allowing her to think of such a thing as marriage. Please under-stand distinctly that I should be not a whit more ready to listen to such a request from any other man—older or younger, richer or poorer."

"But she is well worth waiting for, sir, and if you would only let me speak to her and try to win her affections, I—"

"That must be waited for, too, Frank. I cannot and will not have her approached upon the subject," was the almost stern rejoinder. "Promise me that you will not do or say anything to give her the idea that you want to be more to her than a friend."

"That is a hard thing you are requiring, sir," sighed Frank.

"But quite necessary if you would be permitted to see much of Gracie," returned the captain with great decision. "And, seeing that you feel toward her as you have just told me you do, I think the less you see of each other—the better. Should she be in good, firm health some six or eight years hence, and you and she then have a fancy for each other, her father will not, probably, raise any objection to your suit. But until then, I positively forbid anything and everything of the kind."

"I must say I find that a hard sentence, captain," sighed the would-be suitor. "It strikes me that most fathers would be a trifle more ready to make an eli-gible match for a daughter of Miss Gracie's age. She is very young, I acknowledge, but I have known some girls to marry even younger. And will you not even allow her to enter into an engagement?"

"No. I have no desire at all to rid myself of my daughter—very far from it. For my first set of children, I hold on to a particularly tender feeling because—excepting each other—they have no very near relative but myself. They were quite young when they lost their mother, and for years I have felt that I must fill to them the place of both parents as far as possible, and I have tried to do so. As one result," he added with his pleasant smile, "I find that I am exceedingly loath to give them up into any other care and keeping."

"But since we are both neighbors and distant connections, and my brother is also engaged to Miss Lu, you do not absolutely forbid me to visit your house? Do you, sir?"

"No. You may see Gracie in my presence—perhaps occasionally out of it—provided you carefully obey my injunction to refrain from anything like courting. Do you understand?

"Thank you, sir. I accept the conditions," was Frank's response, and the two separated just as Lucilla and Gracie appeared at the top of the stairway near which they had been standing. Frank passed out onto the veranda, and the captain moved slowly in the opposite direction.

"There's father now!" exclaimed Gracie, tripping down the stairs. "Papa," as he turned at the sound of her voice and glanced up at her, "I've been rearranging my hair. Please tell me if you like it in this style."

"Certainly, daughter. I like it in any style in which I have ever seen it arranged," he returned, regarding it critically but with an evidently admiring gaze. "I am glad and thankful that you have an abundance of it—such as it is," he added sportively, taking her hand in his as she reached his side.

Then turning to Lucilla, "And yours, too, Lulu, seems to be in well-cared-for condition."

"Thank you, papa, dear. I like occasionally to hear you call me by that name so constantly used in the happy days of my childhood."

"Ah! I hope that does not mean that these are not happy days?" he said, giving her a look of kind and fatherly scrutiny.

"Oh, no, indeed, father! I don't believe there is a happier girl than I in all this broad land."

"I am thankful for that," he said with a tenderly affectionate look into her eyes as she stood gazing up into his. "There is nothing I desire more than the happiness of these two, dear daughters of mine."

"Yes, father dear, we both know you would take any amount of trouble for our pleasure or profit," said Gracie merrily. "But just to know that we belong to you is enough for us. Isn't it, Lu?"

"And are dear to him," added Lucilla. "I couldn't be the happy girl I am if I didn't know that."

"Never doubt it, my darlings, never for a moment," he said in a moved tone.

"Oh, so here you are, girls!" exclaimed a familiar voice just to their rear. "I have been all around the veranda looking for you, but you seemed to be lost in the crowd or to have vanished into thin air."

"Certainly not that last, sister Rose," laughed the captain. "I am happy to say there is something a good deal more substantial than that about them."

"Yes, I see there is. Both are looking remarkably well. And now I hope we can have a good chat. There has hardly been an opportunity for it yet—there being such a crowd of relations and friends and such a commotion over the wedding—and you know I want to hear all about what you did and saw in Florida. I also want to tell you of the improvements we are talking of making at Riverside."

"You will have hardly time for a very long talk, Rosie," said her mother, joining them at that moment. "The call to dinner will come soon, but here are some comfortable chairs and a sofa in which you can rest and chat until then."

"Yes, mamma. You will join us, will you not? And you, too, brother Levis?" as the captain turned toward the outer door.

"I shall be pleased to do so if my company is desired," he replied, taking a chair near the little group already seated.

"Of course, it is, sir. I have always enjoyed your company even when you were my respected and revered instructor with the right and power to punish me if I failed in conduct or recitation," returned Rosie in the bantering tone she had so often adopted in days gone by.

"I am rejoiced to hear it," he laughed.

"And you may as well make yourself useful as storyteller of all you folks saw and did in Florida," she continued.

"Much too long a tale for the few minutes we are likely to be able to give to it at present," he said. "Let us reserve that for another time and now hear the story of your own changes at Riverside."

"Or we could talk about this morning's wedding. It was a pretty one. Wasn't it? I never saw Sydney look so charming as she did in that wedding gown and veil. I hope they will have as pleasant a wedding trip as my Will and I had and be as happy afterward as we are."

"I hope so, indeed," said her mother, "and that their after life may be a happy and prosperous one, as well."

"Yes, mamma, I join you in that. And, Lu, how soon do you expect to follow suit and give her the right to call you sister?"

"When my father bids me and not a moment sooner," replied Lucilla, turning an affectionately smiling look upon him.

He returned it, saying, "Which will not be for many months to come. He is far from feeling ready to resign even one of his heart's best treasures."

"Oh, it is a joy to have you call me that, papa!" she exclaimed low and feelingly.

They chatted on for a few minutes longer when they were interrupted by the call to the dinner table. It was a very welcome one, for the sports had given good appetites, and the viands were toothsome and delicious. The meal was not eaten in haste or silence but amid cheerful, mirthful chat and low-toned, musical laughter. With its numerous courses, it occupied more than an hour.

On leaving the banqueting room, they again scattered about the parlors, verandas, and grounds, resuming the intimate and friendly interaction held there before the summons to their feast.

Captain Raymond had kept a watchful eye upon his daughters—Gracie especially—and now took pains to seat her near himself on the veranda, saying, "I want you to rest here a while, daughter, for I see you are looking weary, which is not strange, considering how much more than your usual amount of exercise you have already taken today."

"Yes, I am a little tired, papa," she answered with a loving smile up into his eyes as she sank somewhat wearily into the chair. "It is very pleasant to have you so kindly careful of me."

"Ah!" he returned, patting her cheek and smiling affectionately upon her. "It behooves everyone to be careful of his own particular treasures."

"And our dear Gracie is certainly one of those," said Violet, coming to the other side of the young girl and looking down a little anxiously into the sweet, fair face. "Are you very weary, dearest?"

"Oh, not so very, mamma dear," she answered blithely. "This is a delightful chair papa has put me into, and a little rest in it, while digesting the good, hearty meal I have just eaten, will make me all right again, I think."

"Won't you take this other one by my side, my love? I think you, too, need a little rest," said the captain gallantly.

"Thank you, I will, if you will occupy that one on her other side, so that we will have her between us. And here come Lu and Rosie, so that we can perhaps finish the chat she tells me she was holding with you and the girls before the call to dinner."

"I don't believe we can, mamma," laughed Gracie. "Here come Will Croly and Chester to take possession of them — Eva and Max, too, and Frank."

"Then we will just defer it until another time," said Violet. "Those who have children will soon be leaving for their homes, and those left behind will form a smaller, quieter party."

Violet's surmises proved correct, those with young children presently taking their departure in order that their little ones might seek their nests.

The air began to grow cool, and the family and remaining guests found it now pleasanter within doors than upon the verandas. Music and conversation made the time pass rapidly, a light tea was served, Grandpa Dinsmore read a portion of Scripture and led in a short prayer, a little chat followed, and the remaining guests bade adieu for the present and went their ways. Maud's two brothers and the Dinsmores from the Oaks were among the departing party.

"Now, Gracie, my child, linger not a moment longer, but get to bed as fast as you can," said Captain Raymond to his second daughter as they stood upon the veranda, looking after the departing guests. His tone was tenderly affectionate, and he gave her a goodnight caress as he spoke.

"I will, father dear," she answered cheerfully and made haste to do his bidding.

"She is looking very weary. I fear I have let her exert herself today far more than was for her good," he remarked somewhat anxiously to his wife and Lucilla standing near.

"But I hope a good night's rest will make it all right with her," Violet returned in a cheery tone, adding playfully. "We certainly have plenty of doctors at hand, if anything should go wrong with her or any of us."

"Excellent ones, too," said Lucilla. "But I hope and really expect that a good night's rest will quite restore her to her usual health and strength. So, father, don't feel anxious and troubled."

"I shall endeavor not to, my wise young mentor," he returned with a slight laugh, laying a hand lightly upon her shoulder as he spoke.

"Oh, papa, please do excuse me if I seemed to be trying to teach you!" she exclaimed in a tone of penitence. "I'm afraid it sounded very conceited and disrespectful of me."

"If it did, it was not, I am sure, so intended. So I shall not punish you this time," he replied in a tone that puzzled her with the question whether he was jesting or in earnest.

"I hope you will if you think I deserve it, father," she said low and humbly, Violet having left them and gone within doors and no one else being near enough to overhear her words.

At that, he put his arm about her and drew her closer. "I but jested, daughter," he said in tender tones. "I am not in the least displeased with you. So your only punishment shall be an order presently to go directly to your room and prepare for bed. But first let us have our usual bit of bed-time chat, which I believe I enjoy as fully as does my little girl herself."

"Oh, father, how kind of you to say that!" she exclaimed in low but joyous tones. "I do dearly love to make you my confidant. You are so wise and kind, and I am so sure that you love me dearly, as your very own God-given property. Am I not that still as truly as I ever was?"

"Indeed you are! As truly now as when you were a babe in arms," he said with a happy laugh, drawing her closer to his heart. "A treasure that no amount of money could buy from me. Your price is above rubies, my own darling."

"What sweet words, papa!" she exclaimed with a happy sigh. "Sometimes when I think of all my past naughtiness—giving you so much pain and trouble—I wonder that you can love me half so well as you do."

"Dear child, I think I never loved you the less because of all that, nor you me less because of the severity of my discipline."

"Papa, I believe I always loved you better for your strictness and severity. You made it so clear to me that it was done for my own good and that it hurt you when you felt it your duty to inflict pain."

"It did, indeed!" he said. "But for a long time now, my eldest daughter has been to me only joy — a comfort, a delight — so that I can ill bear the thought of resigning her to another."

"Ah, father, what sweet, sweet words to hear from your lips! They make me so glad, so happy."

"Pleasant words those are for me to hear, and a pleasant thought it is that my dear, eldest daughter is not in haste to leave my protecting care for that of another. I trust Chester is inclined to wait patiently until the right time comes?"

"He has made it evident to me that he would much rather shorten the time of waiting if there were a possibility of gaining my father's consent."

"But that there is not," the captain replied with decision. "If I should consider only my own feeling and inclination and my belief as to what would be really best for you, I should certainly keep full possession of my eldest daughter for several years to come. I have had a talk with Dr. Conly on the subject, and he, as a physician, tells me it would be far better in most cases for a girl to remain single until well on toward twenty-five."

"Which would make her quite an old maid, I should think, papa," laughed Lucilla. "Yet, if you bid me wait that long and can make Chester content, I'll not be at all rebellious."

"No, I don't believe you would, Lulu, but I have really no idea of trying you so far. By the way, Rosie and her Will as well as Maud and Dick seem to be two very happily married couples. What do you think?"

"Yes, indeed, father. It is a pleasure to watch them. And do you know I think Frank Dinsmore is casting longing eyes at our Gracie."

"But you don't think the dear child cares at all for him. Do you?"

"Oh, no, sir! No, indeed! Gracie doesn't care in the least for beaux and loves no other man half so well as she does her father and mine."

"Just as I thought, but I want you quietly to help me prevent any private interviews between them—lest she might learn to care for him."

"Thank you for trusting me, papa. I will do my best," she responded.

Then they bade goodnight, and Lucilla went to her room. She found Eva there, and they chatted pleasantly together as they prepared for bed. Eva had noticed Frank's evident devotion to Gracie and spoke of it, adding, "It is a pity, for, of course, your father—I had very nearly said father, for I begin to feel as if I belonged to his flock—considering us older ones too young to marry, will say she is very far from being old enough for that sort of attention."

"Yes, he does," replied Lucilla. "And I want your help in a task he has set for me—the endeavor to keep them from being alone together."

"I'll do so with pleasure," laughed Evelyn. "But I think probably it would be just as well to take

Gracie herself into the plot, for I feel very sure in saying that she doesn't care a pin for Frank but dotes upon her father."

CHAPTER FIFTEENTH

THE LADIES OF THE Torriswood party retired for the night almost immediately on their arrival there, but the gentlemen lingered a little in the room used by Dr. Percival as his office. There was some cheerful chat over the events of the day in which Frank Dinsmore took no part. He sat in moody silence, seeming scarcely to hear what the others were saying.

"What's the matter with you, Frank?" queried the doctor at length. "Didn't things go off to suit you at all today?"

"Well enough," grumbled Frank, "except that I don't seem to be considered as worthy as my brother is of being taken into—well, let's just say, a certain family really no better than my own, unless in regard to wealth."

"Oh, ho! So that's the way the land lies! It's Gracie Raymond you're after, eh? She won't consent?"

"Her father won't, and I must not say a word to her on the subject."

"And he is right, Frank," returned the doctor gravely. "She is far too young and too delicate to begin with such things. Art would tell you that in a moment, if you should ask him. My opinion as a physician is that marriage now would be likely to kill her within a year, or, if she lived, make her an invalid for life."

"I'd be willing to let marriage wait if I might only speak and win her promise, but no, I'm positively forbidden to say a word."

"You would gain nothing by it if you did," said Chester. "She is devoted to her father and hasn't the least idea of falling in love with any other man."

"Ridiculous!" growled Frank. "Well, things being as they are, I'll not tarry long in this part of the country. I'll go back and attend to the business of our clients, and you, Chester, can stay on here with your fiancée and her family and perhaps gather up a larger amount of health and strength."

"Don't be in a hurry about leaving us, Frank," said Dick cordially. "Maud has been calculating on at least a few days more of your good company, and there's no telling when you may find it convenient to pay us another visit."

"Thanks, Dick. You are hospitality itself, and this is a lovely home you have secured for yourself and Maud. I'll sleep on the question of the time of departure. Now goodnight and pleasant dreams. I hope none of your patients will call you out before sunrise."

And with that they separated, each to seek his own sleeping apartment.

For some hours all was darkness and silence within and without the house. Then the doctor was awakened by the ringing of his night bell.

"What is wanted?" he asked, going at once to the open window.

"You, doctah, fast as you kin git dar, down to Lamont—ole Massa Gest's place. Leetle Miss Nellie, she got a fit."

"Indeed! I am very sorry to hear t. I'll be there as soon as possible," and turning from the window, the doctor rang for his servant, ordered horses saddled and brought to a side door, then hurried on his clothes, explaining matters to the now awakened Maud as he did so. He gathered up the remedies likely to be needed and hastened away.

Directing his servant to keep close in his rear, he rode rapidly in the direction of the place named by the messenger. He found the child very ill and not fit to be left by him until early morning.

It was in the darkest hour, just before day, that he started for home again. All went well till he was within a few rods of home, but then his horse—a rather wild, young animal—took fright at the hoot of an owl in a tree close at hand, reared suddenly, and threw him violently to the ground. Then the horse rushed away in the direction of his stable.

"Oh, doctah, sah, is you hurt bad?" queried the servant, hastily alighting and coming to his master's side.

"Pretty badly, I am afraid, Pete," groaned the doctor. "Help me to the house, and then you must ride over to Viamede as fast as you can, wake up Dr. Harold Travilla, and ask him to come to me immediately to set some broken bones. Take one of the other horses with you for him to ride. Oh," as he attempted to rise, "I'm hardly able to walk, Pete. You'll have to pretty nearly carry me to the house."

"I kin do dat. Ise strong-built. You jes lemme tote you 'long like de mammies do de leetle darlins."

And with that, Pete lifted Dr. Percival in his arms, carried him to the house and on up to his own sleeping room, where he laid him gently down upon his bed in an almost fainting condition.

Maud was greatly alarmed and bade Pete hasten with all speed for one of the doctor cousins.

"Harold, Harold!" groaned the sufferer. "He is older than Herbert and nearer than Art, who is at the Parsonage. And he can bring Herbert with him should he see fit."

Pete, alarmed at the condition of his master, to whom he had become strongly attached, made all the haste he could to bring the needed help, but the sun was already above the tree tops when he reached Viamede.

The first person he saw there was Captain Raymond, who had just stepped out upon the veranda as was his usual habit.

"Morning, sah! Is you uns one ob de doctahs?" he queried in anxious tones, as he reined in his horse at the foot of the veranda steps.

"No," replied the captain. "But there are doctors in the house. You are from Torriswood, I think. Is any one ill there?"

"Massa doctah, he's 'most killed! Horse frowed him. Please, sah, where de doctahs? I'se in pow'ful big hurry to git dem dere fore—"

"Here," called the voice of Harold from an upper window. "Is it I that am wanted? I'll be down there in five minutes or less."

"Yes, I think it is you and probably Herbert also, who are wanted in all haste at Torriswood," answered Captain Raymond, his voice betraying both anxiety and alarm. "It seems Dick has met with a serious accident and has sent for one or both of you."

"Yes," replied Herbert, speaking as Harold had from the window, "we will both go to him as speedily as possible and do what we can for his relief. Please, captain, order another horse saddled and brought around immediately."

The captain at once complied with the request, and in very few minutes both doctors were riding briskly toward Torriswood. They found their patient in much pain from a dislocated shoulder and some broken bones—all of which they proceeded to set as promptly as possible. But there were some symptoms of internal injury that occasioned more alarm than the displacement and fracture of the bones. They held a consultation outside of the sick room.

"I think we should have Cousin Arthur here," said Harold. "'In a multitude of counselors is safety,' Solomon tells us, and Art excels us both in wisdom and experience."

"Certainly," responded Herbert. "Let us summon him at once. I am very glad, indeed, that he is still within reach."

"As I am. I will speak to Maud and have him sent for immediately."

A messenger was promptly dispatched to the Parsonage and returned shortly, bringing Dr. Conly with him. Another examination and consultation followed, and Dr. Percival, who had become slightly delirious, was pronounced in a critical condition. Yet the physicians, though anxious, by no means despaired of his ultimate recovery.

The news of the accident had by this time reached all of the connection in that neighborhood, and silent petitions on his behalf were going up from many hearts. On behalf of his young wife also, for poor Maud seemed well nigh distracted with grief and the fear of the bereavement that threatened her.

Mrs. Embury, too, was greatly distressed, for Dick and she had been all their lives a devotedly attached brother and sister. No day now passed in which she did not visit Torriswood that she might catch a sight of his dear face and learn as far as possible his exact state. Though neither her nursing nor that of the other loving relatives was needed—the doctors and an old servant, skilled in that line of work, were doing all that could be done for his relief and comfort.

Mrs. Betty Norton, his half-sister, was scarcely less pained and anxious—as were Maud's brothers and all the relatives in that region.

It was from her father Lucilla first heard of the accident when she joined him on the veranda at Viamede directly after the departure of the doctors and Pete for Torriswood.

"Oh, father!" she exclaimed. "I do hope he is not seriously injured! Poor Maud! She must be sorely distressed, for he has proved such a good, kind husband, and she almost idolizes him."

"Yes, I feel deeply for her as well as for him. We will pray for them both, asking that if it be consistent with the will of God, he may be speedily restored to perfect health and strength."

"Yes, papa. What a comfort it is that we may cast upon the Lord all our cares for ourselves and others!"

"It is, indeed! I have found it so in many a sore trial sent to myself or to some one dear to me. I am glad for Maud that she has her brothers with her right now."

"I, too, papa, and I suppose Chester will stay with her today."

"Most likely, and my daughter must not feel hurt should he not show himself here at his usual early hour or even at all today."

"I'll try not to, papa. I am sure it would be very selfish of me to grudge poor, dear Maud any show of sympathy or any comfort she might receive from him—her own dear, eldest brother."

"Yes, so I think," said her father. "And I should not expect it of any one of my daughters."

Chester came at length, some hours later than his wont, looking grave and troubled. In answer to inquiries, "Yes, poor Dick is certainly badly hurt," he said. "Maud is well-nigh distracted with grief and anxiety. She is a most devoted wife and considers him her all."

"But the case is not thought to be hopeless?" Mr. Dinsmore asked.

"No, not exactly that, but the doctors are not able yet to decide just what the internal injury may be."

"And while there is life there is hope," said Grandma Elsie in determinately cheerful tones. "It is certainly in his favor that he is a strong, healthy man in the prime of life.

"And still more that he is a Christian man. Therefore, he is ready for any event," added her father.

"And so loved and useful a man that we may well unite in prayer for his recovery if consistent with the will of God," said Captain Raymond.

"And so we will," said Cousin Ronald. "I feel assured that no one of us will refuse or neglect the performance of that duty."

"And we can plead the promise, 'If two of you shall agree on earth as touching anything that they shall ask, it shall be done for them of My Father which is in heaven,'" said Mrs. Dinsmore. "So I have strong hope that dear Dick will be spared us. He is certainly a much loved and very useful man."

"And Maud must be relieved as far as possible from other cares," remarked Mrs. Travilla. "I shall at once invite my brother and his family here. There is room enough, especially as my two sons are there and will be nearly, if not all, the time Dick is so ill."

"No, thank you, cousin," said Chester. "We thank you very much, but Cousin Sue is making herself very useful and could not be well spared. She has undertaken the housekeeping, leaving Maud to devote herself entirely to Dick."

"Oh, that is good and kind of her," was the quick response from several voices.

"And very fortunate it is that she happened to be there, ready for the undertaking," said Mrs. Rose Croly. "If Dick had to have that accident, he couldn't have found a better time for it than now, while there are three good doctors at hand to attend to him."

"True enough," assented Chester. "Things are never so bad but they might be worse."

Days of anxiety and suspense followed, during which Dr. Percival's life seemed trembling in the balance. Drs. Harold and Herbert scarcely left the house and spent much of their time in the sick room, while Dr. Conly made several visits every day, sometimes remaining for hours. The rest of the relatives and near friends came and went with kind offers and inquiries, doing all in their power to show sympathy and give help, while carefully avoiding unwelcome intrusion or disturbance of the quiet that brooded over Torriswood and seemed essential under the circumstances. Nothing was neglected that could be done for the restoration of the loved sufferer, and not one of the many relatives and connections there felt willing to leave the neighborhood while his life hung in the balance.

Chester spent a part of each day with his extremely distressed and anxious sister and a part with his betrothed, from whom he felt very unwilling to absent himself for even one whole day.

The young people and some of the older ones made little excursions, as before, on the bayou and about the woods and fields, Captain Raymond and Violet usually forming a part of the company, especially if his daughter Gracie and Frank Dinsmore were in it.

At other times they gathered upon the veranda or in the parlors and entertained each other with conversation, music, or games of the quiet and innocent kind.

In the meantime, many earnest prayers were sent up on behalf of the injured one — the beloved physician — in the closet, in the family worship, and in the sanctuary when they assembled there on the Sabbath day. And many a silent petition went up as one and another thought of him on his bed of suffering. They prayed in faith, believing that if it were best in the sight of Him who is all-wise and all-powerful and with Whom there is no variableness or shadow of turning, their petition would be granted.

And at length so it proved. The fever left him, consciousness and reason were restored, and presently the rejoicing physicians were able to declare the danger past and the recovery certain should nothing occur to cause a relapse.

Then there was great rejoicing among those who were of his kith and kin and those to whom he was the beloved physician. Then such as were needed at their places of residence presently bade farewell and departed for their homes — Drs. Conly and Herbert Travilla among them, leaving Dr. Harold in sole charge of the invalid.

Those who had come on the *Dolphin* decided to return on it, though they would linger somewhat longer—no one feeling it a trial to have to delay for days or weeks where they were.

Frank Dinsmore was one of the earliest to leave, and Chester, finding that more Southern climate beneficial to him at that season of the year, was entirely willing to entrust the business of the firm to his brother for a time.

So, relieved of anxiety in regard to Dick and still numerous enough to make a very pleasant party, the time passed swiftly and most agreeably to them—especially to the two affianced pairs and the children. Cousin Ronald and Max now and then entertained them by the exertion of their ventriloquial powers. The young people from Magnolia Hall were often with them, and their presence added zest to the enjoyment of little Elsie and Ned in the fun made by their indulgent ventriloquists.

One afternoon, after playing romping games upon the lawn until weary enough to enjoy a quiet rest on the veranda where the older people were, they had hardly seated themselves when they heard a sound of approaching footsteps and a voice that seemed like that of a little girl, asking, "Dear little ladies and gentlemen, may I sit here with you for a while? I'm lonesome and would be glad of some good company, such as I am sure yours must be."

Some of the children, hearing the voices but not able to see the speaker, seemed struck dumb with great surprise.

It was Violet who answered, "Oh, yes, little girl. Please take this empty chair by me and tell me who you are."

"Oh, madam, I really can't tell you my name," answered the voice, now seeming to come from the empty chair by Violet's side. "It seems an odd thing to happen, but there are folks who do sometimes forget their own name."

"And that is the case with you now, is it?" laughed Violet. "Your voice sounds like a little girl, but I very much doubt if you belong to our sex."

"Isn't that rather insulting, madam?" asked the voice in an offended tone.

"Oh, I know you're not a girl or a woman either!" cried Ned Raymond gleefully, clapping his hands and laughing with delight. "You're a man, just pretending to be a little girl."

"That is insulting, you rude little chap, and I shall just go away," returned the voice in indignant tones followed immediately by the sound of footsteps starting from the chair beside Violet and gradually dying away in the distance.

"Why, she went off in a hurry, and I couldn't see her at all!" exclaimed one of the young visitors. Then, as everybody laughed, "Oh, of course it was Cousin Ronald or Cousin Max!"

"Why, the voice sounded to me like that of a little girl," said Violet, "and Cousin Ronald and Max are men."

"Of course they are, but they could talk in the sweet tones of my little girl," said a rough, masculine voice that seemed to come from the doorway into the hall.

Involuntarily nearly everybody turned to look for the speaker, but he was not to be seen.

"And who are you and your girl?" asked another voice, seeming to speak from the farther end of the veranda.

"People of consequence, whom you should treat with courtesy," answered the other, who seemed to stand in the doorway.

"As we will if you will come forward and show yourselves," laughed Lucilla, putting up her hand as she spoke to drive away a bee that seemed to buzz about her ears.

"Never mind, Lu. Its sting won't damage you very seriously," said Max, giving her a look of grand amusement.

"Oh, hark! Here come the soldiers again!" exclaimed Elsie Embury, as the notes of a bugle, quickly followed by those of the drum and fife, seemed to come from a distant point on the farther side of the bayou.

"Don't be alarmed, miss. American soldiers don't harm ladies," said the voice from the farther end of the veranda.

"No, I am not at all alarmed," she returned with a look of amusement directed first at Cousin Ronald, then at Max. "I am not in the least afraid of them."

The music continued for a few minutes, all listening silently to it. Then, as the last strain died away, a voice spoke in tones apparently trembling with affright, "Oh, please somebody hide me! Hide me quick! Quick! Before those troops get here. I'm falsely accused, and who knows but they may shoot me down on sight?"

The speaker was not visible, but from the sounds he seemed to be on the lawn and very near at hand.

"Oh, run around the house and get the servants to hide you in the kitchen or one of the cellars," cried Ned, not quite able, in the excitement of the moment, to realize that there was not a stranger there who might be really in sore peril.

"Thanks!" returned the voice, and a sound as of some one running swiftly in the prescribed direction accompanied and followed the word.

Then the tramp, tramp, as of soldiers on the march, and the music of the drum and fife seemed to draw nearer and nearer.

"Why, it's real, isn't it?" exclaimed one of the children, jumping up and trying to get a nearer view of the approaching troops.

"Oh, don't be afraid," laughed Gracie. "I'm quite sure they won't hurt us or that poor, frightened man, either."

"No," chuckled Ned. "If he went to the kitchen, as I told him to, he'll have plenty of time to hide before they can get there."

"Sure enough, laddie," laughed Cousin Ronald. "They don't appear to be coming on very fast. I hear no more o' their music or their tramp, tramp. Do you?"

"No, sir, and I won't believe they are real live fellows till I see them."

"Well now, Ned," said Lucilla, "I really believe they are very much alive and kindly making a good deal of fun for us."

"Who, who, who?" came at that instant from among the branches of the tree near at hand—or at least it seemed to come from there.

"Our two ventriloquist friends," replied Lucilla, gazing up into the tree as if expecting to see and recognize the bird.

"Oh, what was that?" exclaimed one of the little girls, jumping up in affright, as the squeak of a mouse seemed to come from the folds of her dress.

"Nothing at all dangerous, my dear one," said Mr. Dinsmore, drawing her into the shelter of his arms. "It is no mouse, really, only a little noise made to sound like one."

"Oh, yes, uncle, I might have known that," she said with a rather hysterical little laugh.

Just then the tramp, tramp was heard again apparently near at hand at one side of the house, where the troops might be concealed by the trees and shrubs, and the music of the drum and fife followed the next moment.

"Oh," cried Ned, "won't they catch that fellow who just ran around to the kitchen as I told him to?"

"If they do, I hope they won't hurt him badly," laughed Lucilla.

The music seemed to arouse the anger of several dogs belonging on the place, and at that moment, they set up a furious barking. The music continued and seemed to come nearer and nearer, and the dogs barked more and more furiously. But presently the drum and fife became silent, the dogs ceased barking, and all was quiet. But not for long. The voice that had asked for a hiding place spoke again close at hand.

"Here I am, safe and sound, thanks to the little chap who told me where to hide. The fellows didn't find me, and I'm off. But if they come here looking for me, please don't tell which way I've gone. Good-bye, then, and thank you."

"Wait a minute and tell us who you are before you go," called out Eric Leland, and from the tree came the owl's, "Who, who, who?"

"Who I am?" returned the manlike voice, seeming to speak from a greater distance. "Well, sir, that's for me to know, and you to find out."

"Please tell us which of you it was—Max or Cousin Ronald," said Ned, looking from one to the other.

"That's for us to know, and you to find out, little brother," laughed Max.

"Papa," said Ned, turning to his father, "I wish you'd order Max to tell."

"Max is of age now and not at present under my orders," replied Captain Raymond with a humorous look and smile. And just then came the call to the tea table.

Ned was unusually quiet during the meal, gazing scrutinizingly every now and then at his father or Max. When they had returned to the veranda, he watched his opportunity and seized upon a moment when he could speak to his brother without being overheard by anyone else.

"Brother Max," he queried, "won't you ever have to obey papa any more?"

"Yes, little brother," returned Max, looking slightly amused. "I consider it my duty to obey papa now whenever it pleases him to give me an order. And it will be my duty as long as he and I both live."

"And you mean to do it?"

"Yes, indeed."

"So do I," returned Ned with great decision. "And I think all our sisters do, too. Because the Bible tells us to, and besides papa knows best about everything. Doesn't he, Max?"

"Very true, Ned, and I hope none of us will ever forget that or fail to obey his orders or wishes or to follow his advice."

* * *

CHAPTER SIXTEENTH

DR. PERCIVAL HAD so far recovered as to be considered able to lie in a hammock upon an upper veranda where he could look out upon the beauties of the lawn, the bayou, and the fields and woods beyond. Dr. Harold Travilla was still in attendance and seldom left him for any great length of time. He was never alone and seldom with only the nurse—Maud, one of Dick's sisters, or some other relative being always near at hand ready to wait upon him, chat pleasantly for his entertainment, or remain silent as seemed best to suit his mood at the moment.

He was patient, cheerful, and easily entertained, but he did not usually talk very much himself.

One day he and Harold were alone for a time. Both had been silent for some moments when Dick, turning an affectionate look upon his cousin, said in grateful tones, "How very good, kind, and attentive you have been to me, Harold. I think that but for you and the other two doctors—Cousins Arthur and Herbert—I should now be lying under the sod. I must acknowledge that you are a most excellent physician and surgeon," he added with an appreciative smile, holding out his hand.

Harold took the hand and, pressing it rather affectionately in both of his, said with feeling, "Thank you, Dick. I consider your opinion worth a great deal, and it is a joy to me that I have been permitted to aid in helping on your recovery. But I am no more deserving of thanks than the others. Indeed both Herbert and I felt it to be a very great help to be able to call Cousin Arthur in to give his opinion, advice, and assistance, which he did freely and faithfully. He is an excellent physician and surgeon—as I know you to be also—the knowledge of which increases the delight of having been, by God's blessing upon our efforts, able to pull you through, thus saving a most useful life."

"Thank you," replied Dick in a moved tone. "By God's help, I shall try to make it more useful in the future than it has been in the past—should He see fit to restore me to health and vigor. I feel at present as if I might never again be able to walk or ride."

"I think you need change of climate for a while," said Harold. "What do you say to going North with us, if Captain Raymond should give you and Maud an invitation to take passage in his yacht?"

"Why, that is a splendid idea, Harold!" exclaimed Dick with such a look of animation and pleasure as had not been seen upon his features for many a day. "Should I get the invitation and have Bob come back in time to attend to our practice, I—I really shall, I think, be strongly inclined to accept."

"I hope so, indeed," Harold said with a smile. "I haven't a doubt that you will get it. I know of no one who loves better than the captain to give pleasure. Speak of angels! Here he is with his wife and yours," as just at that moment the three stepped out from the open doorway upon the veranda.

"The three of us, Harold? Are we all angels today?" asked Violet with a smile, stepping forward and taking Dick's hand in hers.

"Quite as welcome as if you were, cousin," said Dick. "Ah, captain! It was you we were speaking of at the moment of your arrival."

"Ah? A poor substitute for an angel, I fear," was the rejoinder in the captain's usual pleasant tones. "But I hope it was the thought of something that may be in my power to do for you, Cousin Dick."

"Thank you, captain. You are always most kind," returned Dick, asking Harold by a look to give the desired explanation. He did so at once by repeating what had just passed between him and Dr. Percival in regard to a northern trip to be taken by the latter upon his partner's return from his bridal trip.

Captain Raymond's countenance brightened as he listened and scarcely waiting for the conclusion, "Why, certainly," he said. "It will be an easy matter to make room for Cousins Dick and Maud and a delight to have them with us on the voyage and after we reach home until the warm weather sends us all farther North for the summer."

"Oh, delightful!" cried Maud. "Oh, Dick, my dear, it will set you up as nothing else could, and you may hope to come back in the fall as well and as strong as ever."

Dr. Percival looked inquiringly at Violet.

"Yes, cousin," she said with a smile. "I think we can make you very comfortable without inconveniencing anybody, especially as Grandpa and Grandma Dinsmore decline to return in the *Dolphin*. They go from here to Philadelphia by rail to visit her relations there or in that region. So you need not hesitate about it for a moment, and," glancing at her brother, "you will have your doctor along to see that you are well taken care of and not allowed to expose yourself on deck when you should be down in the salon or lying in your berth."

"Yes," laughed Harold. "I shall do my best to keep my patient within bounds and see that he does nothing to bring on a relapse and so do discredit to my medical and surgical knowledge and skill."

"Which I should certainly be most sorry to do," smiled Dick. "If I do not do credit to it all, it shall be no fault of mine. Never again, cousin, can I for a moment forget that you stand at about the head of your profession—or deserve to, certainly—as both physician and surgeon. Captain, I accept your kind offer with most hearty thanks. I feel already something like fifty per cent better for the very thought of the rest and pleasure of the voyage, the visit to my old home and friends, and then a sojourn during the hot months in the cooler regions of the North."

From that time, his improvement was far more rapid than it had been, and Maud was very happy over that and her preparations for the contemplated trip, in which Grandma Elsie and Cousins Annis and Violet gave her valuable assistance.

At length, a letter was received telling that the newly married pair might be expected two days later. Chester brought the news to Viamede shortly after breakfast, and all heard it with pleasure, for they were beginning to feel a strong drawing toward their northern homes.

"It is good news," said Grandma Elsie. "Now I want to carry out a plan I have been thinking of for some time."

"In regard to what?" asked her father.

"The reception to be given our bride and groom," she answered. "I want it to be given here. All the connection now in these parts to be invited, house and lawn to be decorated as they were for our large party just after the wedding, and such a feast of fat things as we had then to be provided."

"That is just like you, mother," said Captain Raymond. "You are always thinking how to give those around you pleasure and how to save trouble for them."

"Ah, it seems to me that I am the one to do it in this instance," she returned with a gratified smile. "I have the most means, the most room of any of the connection about here, an abundance of excellent help as regards all the work of preparation and the entertainment of the guests, and everything that the occasion calls for. Dick and Maud are in no shape to do the entertaining, though I do certainly hope that they may both be able to attend, even if he, poor fellow, can only lie in a hammock on the veranda or under the trees. If they like, they may as well come fully prepared for their journey and start with us from here."

"A most excellent and kind plan, cousin, as yours always are," said Chester, giving Mrs. Travilla a pleased and gratified look. "I have no doubt it will be accepted if Dr. Harold approves."

"As he surely should, since it is his mother's," remarked Violet in her sprightly way. "Suppose you drive over at once, mamma, see the three, and have the whole thing settled."

"A very good idea, I think, Vi," was the smiling rejoinder. "Captain, will you order a carriage to be brought around promptly, and will both you and Vi go with me? You could take Elsie and Ned also, if they would care for a drive," she added, giving the little folks a kindly inquiring look.

Both joyfully accepted the invitation, if papa and mamma were willing, and little Elsie added, "And if Cousin Dick is not well enough for us to go in, we can stay in the carriage or out in the grounds until you are all ready to come back."

"Yes," said her father. "So there is no objection to your going."

"There will still be a vacant seat," said Grandma Elsie. "Will you not go with us also, Gracie? I have heard Harold say driving was good exercise for you."

"Oh, thank you, ma'am," said Gracie. "I should like it very much, if papa approves," glancing with an inquiring smile at him.

"Certainly. I am quite sure that my daughter Gracie's company will add to my enjoyment of the drive," was the captain's kindly response.

"And Grandma Elsie, cannot you find some use for the stay-at-homes?" asked Max. "Chester and myself for instance. Would there be any objection to having 'Old Glory' set waving from the tree tops today?"

"None whatever," she returned with her sweet smile. "I, for one, never weary of seeing it 'wave o'er the land of the free and the home of the brave.'"

"I think anyone who does weary of it isn't worthy to be called an American!" exclaimed Lucilla with warmth.

"Unless one is a *South* American," remarked Eva with a smile. "You would not expect such an one to care for 'Old Glory.'"

"Oh, no, certainly not. It is no more to them than to the rest of the world."

"But I dare say it must mean a good deal to some of the rest of the world, judging from the way they flock to these shores," said Chester.

"Which I sincerely wish some of idle and vicious wouldn't," said Lucilla.

"Honest and industrious ones we are always glad to welcome," said Chester, "but not the idle and vicious. And as our own native born boys must be twenty-one years old before they are allowed to vote, I think every foreigner should be required to wait here that same length of time before receiving the right of suffrage."

"I heartily agree with you in that, Chester," said Captain Raymond.

"Unfortunately, we have far too many selfish politicians—men who are selfishly set upon their own advancement to wealth and power. They seem to care little, if anything, for their country and their country's good, and, in order to gain votes for themselves, they have managed to have the right of suffrage given to those foreigners in order to get into a place of power through them."

"I haven't a particle of respect for such men," exclaimed Lucilla hotly. "And I do not hold much more for some others who are so engrossed in the management of their own affairs—the making of money by such close attention to business—that they can't, or won't, look at all after the interests of their country."

"Very true, my dear sister," said Max with a roguish look and smile. "So it is high time the ladies should be given the right of suffrage. Don't you think so, Lu?"

"The right! I think they have that already," she returned with rising color and an indignant look. "But domineering men won't allow them to use it."

"Why, daughter," laughed the captain, "I had no idea that you held such strong views upon woman's suffrage. Surely it is not the result of my training."

"No, indeed, papa. But you have tried to teach me to think for myself," she returned with a blush and a smile, adding, "It is not just that I am wanting to vote—even if I were old enough, which I know I am not yet—but I do want the laws made and administered by my own countrymen."

"Ah, and that is perhaps the result of my teachings. Are you not afraid, Chester," turning to him, "that one of these days she may prove too independent for you?"

"Ah, captain, if you are thinking of frightening me out of my bargain let me assure you at once that it is perfectly useless," laughed Chester in return.

"Ah, yes. I suppose so," sighed the captain in mock distress. "But I must go now and order the carriage," he added, rising and hastening away in the direction of the stables.

"And we to make your preparations for the drive and call to Torriswood," said Grandma Elsie, addressing Violet and the younger ones expecting to be of the party. "Dick and Maud should have as early a report of our plans and purposes as we can give them."

To that, Violet and Gracie gave a hearty assent, the little ones echoing it joyfully, and by the time the carriage could be brought to the door, they were all ready to enter it.

They found Maud and Dick full of pleasurable excitement, and the former already at work upon her packing. Both Grandma Elsie's plan and invitation were highly appreciated by both and joyfully accepted.

The arrangements were soon made. If all went well with Dr. and Mrs. Johnson, they would reach Viamede the next afternoon, stay there in the enjoyment of its hospitality until toward bedtime of that evening, then come on to Torriswood. A day or two later, the others would start upon their northward journey. They would all go together to New Orleans, Grandpa and Grandma Dinsmore taking the cars there for Philadelphia and the rest starting for home by water along the Gulf of Mexico, around Florida, and up the Atlantic coast.

The whole plan met Dr. Harold's unqualified approval, while Dr. Percival was so charmed with it that he insisted that the very prospect of it all had nearly restored him to health and strength.

"Is that so, cousin?" exclaimed Violet with a pleased laugh. "Then, you will be another Samson by the time we reach our homes."

"Ah, if I can only recover the amount of strength I had before my accident, I shall be satisfied," said he. "I shall know how to appreciate it as I never did in the past."

All the necessary arrangements having now been made, the Viamede party presently returned to their temporary home, which they found looking very bright and patriotic with flags fluttering from tree tops, gables, windows, and verandas. The young folks left behind had been very busy in their work of adornment. The result of their labors met with warm approval from Grandma Elsie, the captain, and Violet. Gracie and Elsie Raymond, too, expressed themselves as highly pleased, while Ned quite went into raptures at the sight of so fine a display of the *Star-spangled Banner*.

"Now, Cousin Ronald," he exclaimed, turning to Mr. Lilburn, "don't you think it is the very prettiest flag that floats?"

"As bonny a one as ever I saw, laddie," responded the old gentleman with a genial smile. "Don't you know that, having adopted this as my country, I now consider it as truly my ain banner as it is yours?"

"Oh, yes, sir, and I'm glad you do," returned Ned with a pleased look. "I like this to be your country as well as mine."

"It is certainly a grand country, laddie," was the pleasant-toned response. "And it is the native land of my bonny young wife and the dear little bairns of my son Hugh. So I may well give it a good share of my affection."

The weather continued fine, all the preparations were carried forward successfully, and by noon of the next day, the Percivals were ready to enjoy a brief stay at Viamede. Dick was gaining strength, but he was carefully attended and watched over by his cousin Harold. Maud was full of life and happiness because of his improvement and the pleasant prospect before them. It would be so delightful, she thought and said, to see her old home and friends and acquaintances about there, Dick taking his ease among them all for a time, and then to spend some weeks or months farther north, enjoying sea breezes and sun bathing.

All the cousins, older and younger, from Magnolia Hall and the Parsonage were gathered there before the hour when the boat bringing their bride and groom might be expected, and as it rounded to at the wharf, quite a little crowd could be seen waiting to receive them.

The Johnsons had not been apprised of the reception awaiting them and were expecting to go on immediately to Torriswood. But the boat was hailed and stopped by Chester, and at the same time seeing the festive preparations and the assemblage of relatives, they understood what was going on and expected of them. They stepped quickly ashore, where glad greetings were exchanged. Then all moved on to the house where Dr. Percival lay in a hammock on the front veranda.

"Oh, Dick, dear fellow, are you still unable to move about?" asked Dr. Johnson, grasping his hand and looking down into his thin, pale face with eyes filled with tears in spite of himself.

"Oh, I'll soon be all right, Bob. Though if it hadn't been for Harold here," giving the latter a warmly affectionate glance, "I doubt if you would have found a partner in your practice upon your return."

"In that case I am certainly under a very great obligation to you, Harold," Robert said with obvious feeling, as he and Harold grasped hands with cousinly warmth. "You could hardly have done me a greater service."

"Don't talk of obligations," said Harold with emotion. "Dick and you and I are not only all members of the same profession, but we are all near kinsmen. So Dick had a double and strong claim upon me and my services."

"We all think he needs a change," said Maud, standing near. "And so, by Cousin Elsie's kind invitation, we are going with her and the rest in the captain's yacht to visit them and our old homes and then go on farther North to the seashore."

"The very best thing that could be done, I think," said Robert. "It certainly is Dick's turn to have a holiday while I stay and attend to our practice."

The mirth, jollity, and feasting that followed, filling up the rest of the day, were very similar to those of the day of the wedding, weeks before.

Dr. Percival was still feeble, and Mrs. Travilla had some arrangements to make in regard to the conduct of affairs at Viamede after her departure, which together made it best to delay for a few days. But at length all was ready, the good-byes were said, and the return journey to their northern homes was begun.

As had been planned, Mr. and Mrs. Dinsmore took the cars at New Orleans, while the *Dolphin*, bearing the remaining members of their party, passed from west to east along the Gulf of Mexico, around the southern coast of Florida, and up its eastern coast and that of the Carolinas. It was quite a voyage, but it was neither tedious nor tiresome to the passengers, so pleasant did they find each other's society and the variety of books and sports provided for their entertainment.

During the greater part of the voyage, the weather was pleasant enough to allow them to spend the most of their days upon deck, where they could walk about or sit and chat beneath the awnings.

"Grandma," said little Elsie, coming to Mrs. Travilla's side one morning as she sat on deck busied with a bit of fancy work, "would it trouble you to talk to Ned and me a little while?"

"No, dear," was the smiling reply. "But what is it that you wish to hear from me?"

"Something about General Marion, grandma, if you please. I know a little about him and admire him very much, indeed. He was a South Carolina man, I know, and when I heard papa say a while ago that we were on the South Carolina coast, it made me think of Marion. I should be very glad to hear something more of what he did in the Revolution from you."

"And so would I, grandma, ever so much," added Ned, who was close at his sister's side.

"Then sit down, one on each side of me, and I will tell you some things that I have read about General Francis Marion, who was one of the boldest, most energetic, and faithful patriots of the Revolution. He was born in South Carolina in 1732, and it is said he was so small a baby that he might have been easily put into a quart pot."

"He must have had to grow a good deal before he could be a soldier, grandma," laughed Ned.

"Yes, but he had forty-three years in which to do it," said Elsie.

"Yes, Elsie, there were that many years before the Revolutionary War began," said her grandma, "but he was only twenty-seven when he became a soldier by joining an expedition against the Cherokees and other hostile Indian tribes on the western frontier of his state. When the Revolution began, he was made a captain in the second South Carolina regiment. He fought in the battle at Fort Sullivan, on Sullivan's Island, in the contest at Savannah, and many another. He organized a brigade and became a brigadier of the militia of South Carolina. After the battle of Eutaw, he became senator in the Legislature, but he soon went back into the army and remained there till the close of the war."

"Grandma, didn't he and his soldiers camp in the swamps a good deal of the time?" asked Elsie.

"Yes, and they often had only a little food to eat, sometimes sweet potatoes only and but a scant supply of them. A story is told of a young British officer from Georgetown coming to treaty with him regarding prisoners when Marion was camping on Snow's Island at the confluence of the Pee Dee River and Lynch Creek. The Briton was led blindfolded to Marion's camp. There, for the first time, he saw that general—a small man—with groups of his men about him, lounging under the magnificent trees draped with moss. When they had concluded their business, Marion invited the Englishman to dine with him. The invitation was accepted, and great was the astonishment of the guest when the dinner was served—only some roasted potatoes on a piece of bark. 'Surely, general,' he said, 'this cannot be your ordinary fare?' 'Indeed it is,' replied Marion, 'and we are fortunate on this occasion, entertaining company, to have more than our usual allowance.'

"It is said that the young officer then gave up his commission on his return, saying that such a people could not and ought not to be subdued."

"Marion and his men must have really loved their country and liberty to be willing to live in swamps with nothing but potatoes to eat," said Elsie. "It makes me think of the stories I've read about Robin Hood and his merry men."

"Yes," said her grandmother. "Lossing tells us Marion's men were as devoted to him as Robin

Hood's were to their leader. Our poet Bryant has drawn a telling picture of that noble band in his, "Song of Marion's Men:"

"'Our band is few, but true and tried,
    Our leader frank and bold;
The British soldier trembles
    When Marion's name is told.
Our fortress is the good greenwood,
    Our tent the cypress-tree;
We know the forest round us
    As seamen know the sea.
We know its walls of thorny vines,
    Its glades of reedy grass;
Its safe and silent islands
    Within the dark morass.

"'Woe to the English soldiery,
    That little dread us near!
On them shall light at midnight
    A strange and sudden fear;
When, walking to their tents on fire,
    They grasp their arms in vain,
And they who stand to face us
    Are beat to earth again;
And they who fly in terror deem
    A mighty host behind,
And hear the tramp of thousands
    Upon the hollow wind.

"'Then sweet the hour that brings release
    From danger and from toil;
We talk the battle over,
    And share the battle's spoil.
The woodland rings with laugh and shout,
    As if a hunt were up,
And woodland flowers are gather'd
    To crown the soldier's cup.

With merry songs we mock the wind
That in the pine-top grieves,
And slumbering long and sweetly
On beds of oaken leaves.

"'Well knows the fair and friendly moon
The band that Marion leads—
The glitter of their rifles,
The scampering of their steeds.
'Tis life to guide the fiery barb
Across the moonlight plain;
'Tis life to feel the night wind
That lifts his tossing mane.
A moment in that British camp—
A moment—and away
Back to the pathless forest,
Before the peep of day.

"'Grave men there are by broad Santee,
Grave men with hoary hairs;
Their hearts are all with Marion,
For Marion are their prayers.
And lovely ladies greet our band
With kindliest welcoming,
With smiles like those of summer,
With tears like those of spring.
For them we wear these trusty arms,
And lay them down no more
Till we have driven the Briton
Forever from our shore.'"

"And we did drive the British away—or rather
Marion and his men and the rest of our brave soldiers did," exclaimed Ned when the recitation of
the poem was finished. "Didn't they, grandma?"

"Yes, Neddie boy, God helped us to get free and
become the great nation that we are today. To Him
let us give all the glory and the praise."

"Yes, grandma, I know that even those brave and good fighters couldn't have done it if God hadn't helped them. Did he live long after the war was over?"

"About a dozen years, Neddie. He died on the twenty-ninth of February in 1795. We are told his last words were, 'Thank God, since I came to man's estate I have never intentionally done wrong to any man.'"

"And is that all the story about him, grandma?" asked Ned regretfully.

"Enough for the present, I think," replied his grandma. "When you are older, you can read of him in history for yourself. However, some of his work will come in incidentally as I go on with some historical sketches. I want to tell you something of Mrs. Rebecca Motte — one of the brave and patriotic women living in South Carolina at that time — and the doings of the British and Americans on her estate.

"Mrs. Motte was a rich widow. She had a fine large mansion, occupying a commanding position between Charleston and Camden. The British, knowing that she was a patriot, drove her and her family from their home to a farmhouse that she owned that was positioned upon a hill north of her mansion into which they put a garrison of one hundred and fifty men under Captain M'Pherson, a brave British officer.

"Early in May, he was joined by a detachment of dragoons sent from Charleston with dispatches from Lord Rawdon. They were about to leave when Marion and Lee with their troops were seen upon the heights at the farmhouse where Mrs. Motte was living. So the dragoons remained to give their help in the defense of the fort.

"Lee took position at the farmhouse, and his men, with a fieldpiece which General Greene had sent them, were stationed on the eastern slope of the high plain on which Fort Motte stood. Marion at once threw up a mound of dirt and planted a fieldpiece upon it in a position to rake the northern face of the parapet of the fort against which Lee was about to move.

"M'Pherson was without artillery. Between Fort Motte and the height where Lee was posted was a narrow valley, which enabled his men to come within a few yards of the fort. From that, they began to advance by a parallel—a wide trench. By the tenth of the month, they were so far successful that they felt warranted in demanding a surrender. They sent a summons to M'Pherson, but he gallantly refused to comply.

"That evening our men heard that Lord Rawdon had retreated from Camden and was coming in that direction to relieve Fort Motte. The next morning beacon fires could be seen on the high hills of Santee, and that night the besieged were greatly rejoiced to see their gleam on the highest ground of the country opposite Fort Motte. They were delighted but soon found that they had rejoiced too soon.

"Lee proposed a quicker plan for dislodging them than had been thought of before. Mrs. Motte's mansion in the center of their works was covered with a roof of shingles now very dry, as there had been no rain for several days and the heat of the sun had been great. Lee's idea was to set those shingles on fire and so drive the enemy out. He had been enjoying Mrs. Motte's hospitality, and her only marriageable daughter was the wife of a friend of his, so he was very loathe to destroy her property.

But on telling her his plan, he was much relieved to find that she was not only willing but desirous to serve her country by the sacrifice of her property.

"He then told his plan to Marion, and they made haste to execute it. It was proposed to set the roof on fire with lighted torches attached to arrows that should be shot against it. Mrs. Motte, seeing that the arrows the men were preparing to use were not very good, brought out a fine bow and bundle of arrows that had come from the East Indies, and she gave them to Lee.

"The next morning, Lee again sent a flag of truce to M'Pherson, the bearer telling him that Rawdon had not yet crossed the Santee and that immediate surrender would save many lives.

"But M'Pherson still refused, and at noon Nathan Savage, a private in Marion's brigade, shot toward the house several arrows with lighted torches attached. Two struck the dry shingles, and instantly a bright flame was creeping along the roof. Soldiers were sent up to knock off the shingles and put out the fire, but a few shots from Marion's battery raked the loft and drove them below. Then M'Pherson hung out a white flag, the Americans ceased firing, the flames were put out, and at one o'clock the garrison surrendered themselves as prisoners of war.

"Then Mrs. Motte invited both the American and the British officers to a sumptuous dinner that she had made ready for them."

Gracie Raymond had drawn near and was listening in a very interested way to the story as told by Mrs. Travilla.

"Grandma Elsie," she said, as that lady paused in her narrative, "do you remember a little talk between the American and British officers at that dinner of Mrs. Motte's?"

"I am not sure that I do," was the reply. "Can you repeat it for us?"

"I think I can give at least the substance," said Gracie. "One of the prisoners was an officer named Captain Ferguson. He was seated near Colonel Horry, one of our American officers. Addressing him, Ferguson said, 'You are Colonel Horry, I presume, sir?' Horry replied that he was, and Ferguson went on, 'Well, I was with Colonel Watson when he fought your General Marion on Sampit. I think I saw you there with a party of horses and also at Nelson's Ferry, when Marion surprised our party at the house. But I was hid in high grass and escaped. You were fortunate in your escape at Sampit, for Watson and Small had twelve hundred men.'

"'If so,' said Horry, 'I certainly was fortunate, for I did not suppose they had more than half that number.' Then Ferguson said, 'I consider myself equally fortunate in escaping at Nelson's Old Field.'

"'Truly you were,' Horry returned sarcastically. 'For Marion had but thirty militia on that occasion.' The other officers at the table could not refrain from laughing. General Greene afterward asked Horry how he came to affront Captain Ferguson, and Horry answered that he affronted himself by telling his own story.'"

"Ah, I think our soldiers were the bravest," was little Elsie's comment upon that anecdote.

"Yes," said her grandma, "probably because they were fighting for liberty and home."

"Please, grandma tell us another Revolutionary story," pleaded Ned.

"Did you ever hear the story of what Emily Geiger did for the good cause?" asked Grandma Elsie in reply.

"No, ma'am. Won't you please tell it?"

"Yes. Emily was the daughter of a German planter in Fairfield District. She was not more than eighteen years old, but she was very brave. General Greene had an important message to send to Sumter, but because of the danger from the numbers of Tories and British likely to be encountered on the way, none of his men seemed willing to take it. Therefore, he was delighted when this young girl came forward and offered to carry his letter to Sumter. But fearful she might lose it on the way, he made her acquainted with its contents.

"She mounted a fleet horse, crossed the Wateree at the Camden Ferry, and hastened on toward Sumter's camp. On the second day of her journey, while passing through a dry swamp, she was stopped and made prisoner by some Tory scouts, who suspected her because she came from the direction of Greene's army. They took her to a house on the edge of the swamp and shut her up in a room, while they sent for a woman to search her person.

"Emily was by no means willing to have that letter found upon her person, so as soon as she was left alone, she began tearing it up and swallowing it piece by piece. After a while, the woman came and searched her carefully, but she found nothing to incriminate the girl, as the last piece of the letter had already gone down her throat.

"Her captors, now convinced of her innocence, made many apologies and allowed her to go on her way. She reached Sumter's camp, gave him Greene's message, and soon the British under Rawdon were flying before the Americans toward Orangeburg."

"Is that all, grandma?" asked Ned, as Mrs. Travilla paused and glanced up smilingly at Captain Raymond, who now drew near.

"All for the present, Neddie," she replied. "Some other time I may perhaps think of other incidents to give you."

"Ah, mother, so you've been kindly entertaining my children, who are great lovers of stories," remarked the captain. "I hope they have not been too exacting in their entreaties for such amusement?"

"Oh, no," she replied. "They wanted some episodes in the history of the state we are passing, and I have been giving them some accounts of the gallant deeds of General Marion and others."

"A brave, gallant man was Francis Marion, very patriotic and one of the finest characters of that time. He is a countryman of whom we may well be proud," remarked the captain, speaking with earnestness and enthusiasm. "With it all, he was most humane in great contrast to some of the British officers who burnt houses, robbed, and wronged women and children—rendering them shelterless and stripping them of all clothes except those they wore, among even worse acts of barbarity. Bancroft tells us that when the British were burning houses on the Little Pee Dee, Marion permitted his men of that district to go home and protect their wives and families but that he would not suffer retaliation and wrote with truth, 'There is not one house burned by my orders or by any of my people. It is what I detest, to distress poor women and children.'"

"I am proud of him as one of my countrymen," said Gracie. "He was sometimes called 'The Swamp Fox.' Was he not, papa?"

"Yes, the swamps were his usual place of refuge and camping ground."

"I admire him very much and like to hear about him and all he did for our country," said little Elsie. "I am glad and thankful that I didn't live in those dreadful war times."

"As you well may be, my dear child," said her father. "We cannot be too thankful for the liberty we enjoy in these days, which was largely won for us by Marion and other brave and gallant patriots of those darker days. They, and our debt of gratitude to them, should never be forgotten or ignored."

CHAPTER
SEVENTEENTH

THE *DOLPHIN'S* PASSENGERS greatly enjoyed their voyage up the Atlantic coast, yet they were not sorry when they reached their desired haven—the city within a few miles of their homes.

Dr. Percival had gained strength every day and now could go about very well with the help of a friend's arm or a cane. He spent but a part of his time lounging in an easy chair or resting upon a couch.

A telegram had carried to their home friends the information that they expected to reach port on that day, and carriages were there in waiting to convey them to their several places of abode.

Dr. Conly had come for Dr. and Mrs. Percival, as had also Mr. Dinsmore from the Oaks—the one claiming that Roselands was Dick's old home, therefore undoubtedly the proper place for him at present and the other that Maud belonged at the Oaks and, of course, her husband with her. Grandma Elsie had already given them a warm invitation to Ion, and Captain Raymond and Violet the same to Woodburn. It seemed a little difficult to decide who had the prior claim. Dr. Harold said it should be to Ion first in order that he might still have his patient where he could keep continued and careful watch over him. As he grew better and stronger, the others could have their turns at entertaining him and Maud.

To that, Dick laughingly replied that he was now tolerably used to obeying Harold's orders, so he should submit to his decision, still hoping that in time he and Maud might have the pleasure of accepting the other invitations in turn.

That seemed to give everyone a tolerable satisfaction as about as good an arrangement as could well be made.

Both the Beechwood and Woodburn family carriages and Max's pony were there and the carriage from Fairview for Evelyn. Max helped her into it then mounted his steed and rode alongside, the Woodburn carriage driving a little ahead of them, while the other vehicles were somewhat in their rear.

All reached their destinations in safety, each party receiving a joyful welcome on their arrival. Chester, after a brief but affectionate good-bye, "for a short time," to Lucilla, had taken a seat in Mr. Dinsmore's carriage, as he and his brother still made their home at the Oaks. Both pairs of lovers had greatly enjoyed their daily interaction upon the *Dolphin* and gave that up with some feeling of regret, but they comforted themselves with the thought that twenty-four hours would seldom pass without allowing them at least a brief interview.

Bidding good-bye to Eva at the gate into Fairview Avenue, Max rode rapidly onward and entered the Woodburn grounds just in the rear of his father's carriage. He then dismounted at the veranda in time to take part in assisting the ladies and children to alight.

"Oh, how delightful it is to be at home again!" exclaimed Gracie, dancing about and gazing this way and that into the beautifully kept grounds. "I am always glad to go, but still more glad to get back."

"And so am I." "And I," exclaimed the younger ones in turn.

"And I am as glad as anybody else, I think," said Max. "Though I should not be if I were here alone—without father, Mamma Vi, and my sisters and little brother."

"No, indeed! The dear ones make more than half the home," Lucilla said with a loving glance around upon the others then one of ardent affection up into her father's face.

"Yes, indeed," said Gracie. "Father alone is more than half of home to each and every one of us." An assertion that no one was in the least inclined to contradict.

"He certainly is to me—his wife," said Violet, giving him a look that spoke volumes of her respect and love.

"And I certainly know of no man who has less reason to complain of the lack of appreciation by his nearest and dearest," responded the captain in tones slightly tremulous with feeling and a look of fond, proud affection, first at his wife, then at his children, each in turn.

"This is certainly a happy homecoming to us all," said Max, "to me especially, I think, as the one who has seen so little of it for years past. It is to me the dearest spot on earth. Though it would not be without the dear ones it holds."

But housekeeper and servants had now come crowding about with glad greetings, which were warmly returned, and then the family scattered to their rooms to prepare for the dinner just ready to be served.

All of the returned travelers were received with joyful greetings at their homes, not excepting Dr. Harold Travilla at Ion. All there seemed to rejoice that they were to be the first to entertain the cousins—Dr. Percival and Maud. They were very warmly welcomed and speedily installed in the most comfortable quarters—a suite of beautifully furnished apartments on the ground floor, so that Dick might be spared the exertion of going up and down even the easiest flight of stairs. They were more than content.

"We seem to have come into a haven of rest, Maud, my love," Dick remarked, as he lay back in his reclining chair and gazed about with eyes that kindled with joy and admiration.

"Yes, my dear," laughed Maud, "it would seem almost appropriate to put another letter into that noun and call it a heaven—so beautiful and tasteful is everything around us."

"Yes. I wish everybody had as good, kind, capable, and helpful friends and relatives as ours, able to give them such royal entertainment."

"Cousin Elsie is the very person to have large means," said Maud. "For she seems to be always thinking of others and what she can do for their comfort and happiness. There is not a particle of selfishness or self-righteousness about her."

"I heartily agree with you there," said Dick. "I have known her since I was the merest child, and she has always seemed to live to do good and show kindness to all around her. She evidently looks upon her wealth as simply a trust—something the

Lord has put into her hands to be used for His glory and the good of her fellow creatures."

"I am sure you are right about that," said Maud. "And her children resemble her in it. What could have exceeded the kindness of Cousins Harold and Herbert—Cousin Arthur Conly, too—when you were so ill? Oh, Dick dear, I thought I was going to lose you! Oh, how could I ever have borne that?" she added with a sob. "I am sure you and I owe your life to their skillful treatment and their untiring care and devotion."

"We do indeed," he said with emotion. "But for their untiring efforts and God's blessing upon them, I should now be under the sod and my darling a widow," he added tenderly and in quivering tones, drawing her down to give her a fond caress. "How kind Vi and her husband have been," he went on. "The captain is a grand, good man and quite as anxious to use all he has for the glory of God and the good of his fellow creatures as dear Cousin Elsie herself."

"Yes. I don't wonder his wife and children love him so dearly, and I could hardly love him better were he my own brother," said Maud. "I am so glad he and Cousin Violet fancied each other and married when they did."

"Yes, they are the most enjoyable of relatives to us and seem very happy in each other."

Here their bit of chat was interrupted by a tap on the door opening into the hall. Dr. Harold had come to say that dinner was on the table, ask if his patient felt able, and if it would be enjoyable to join the family at their meal.

"Indeed I should like it," was Dick's prompt response. "I think I am entirely equal to the exertion."

"Perhaps even with only your cane, if I give you the support of my arm," suggested Harold.

"Thank you, yes," returned Dick with a pleased look, as Harold assisted him to rise and Maud handed him his cane.

So the little journey was made successfully, and the social meal greatly enjoyed. At its conclusion, Harold assisted Dr. Percival to his couch again, where he lay down just weary enough to take a long, refreshing nap.

On leaving the table, Grandma Elsie went to the telephone and called to Woodburn. Violet answered, "What is it, mother?"

She received this reply, "I would like the whole connection to come here to take tea and spend the evening, and I want you all to come."

The captain, standing near, heard the message also, and as Violet turned inquiringly to him, he said, "Surely there is nothing to prevent any of us from going."

She at once answered, "Thank you, mother, you may expect us all."

The same invitation had been already sent to, and accepted by, the others, and some time before the tea hour they were all there — glad to meet and exchange greetings and chat about all that had occurred since they last saw each other. And Dr. Percival, refreshed and strengthened by his dinner and a long, sound sleep after it, was able to enjoy it all, perhaps as keenly as anyone else. They talked of whatever had occurred among them during the time that they had been separated and of their plans for the coming heated term — who would pass it at home and who go North to find a cooler climate. But it was not necessary to decide fully upon their plans, as some weeks would elapse ere carrying them out, and there would be a good deal of interaction among them in the meantime.

They scattered to their homes early in the evening so that Dr. Percival might not be kept up or awake and that the little ones might be safely and in good season bestowed in their nest for the night.

Dr. Percival improved rapidly in the next few weeks—so rapidly that he was able to make a visit to Roselands, the Oaks, and Woodburn, each in turn. He felt that he should greatly enjoy the journey to the North and the sojourn by the seaside there that awaited him, his wife, and friends.

The two pairs of lovers went quietly and happily on with their courting, considered plans for future house building and housekeeping, and what should be done and enjoyed in the meantime. It seemed but only a little while till they were again on board the *Dolphin* and speeding upon their northward course.

It was the same party that had come in her on that last voyage from the South. Max was still in the enjoyment of his furlough, and by his father's request, he now took command of the vessel. But, the weather being fine throughout the voyage, his duties were not arduous, and Evelyn had no reason to complain of want of attention from her fiancé. Nor had Lucilla, Chester being seldom absent from her side during the day or evening. Captain Raymond began to feel at times that he was already losing—to some extent—his eldest daughter. He sighed over it to himself, but he made no complaint to either of them.

Lucilla's affection for him did not seem to have suffered any abatement, and as had been her custom, she often came to him for a bit of private chat early in the morning or in the evening after the others had gone to their staterooms. In these private interviews, she was the same ardently affectionate daughter she had been for years, so that he felt he had no reason to fear that her betrothed had stolen all of her heart.

But she was very keen sighted as regarded him and his feelings toward her. One evening as, according to his custom, he paced the deck after all the passengers had retired for the night, he heard her light step at his side and her voice asking in its sweetest tones, "Papa dear, mayn't I walk with you for at least a few minutes? I am neither sleepy nor tired, and it is seldom now that I can have my own dear father all to myself."

"Yes, daughter dear," he said, putting an arm about her and caressing her with tenderness. "I am glad to have your company if it is not going to weary you or rob you of needed sleep." Then he drew her hand within his arm, and they paced slowly back and forth, conversing in subdued tones.

"It is so sweet to be alone with you once in a while, my own dear father," she said. "I think, papa, if my engagement has made any changes in my feelings toward you it has been to make you seem to me nearer and dearer, if possible, than ever. Oh, I think it would break my heart if I should ever have to go so far away from you that I could not see and talk with you every day!"

"Dear child, those are sweet words to my ear," he said in moved tones. "I am most thankful that, so far as we can see into the future, there seems little or no danger that we will ever be so separated in this world."

"Yes, papa. That assurance is one of my greatest joys, and I am so glad that my dear father is so strong and well and not so very old," she added with a smile and a look of loving admiration up into his face. "I am not very young, daughter," he returned pleasantly. "Though I think my natural strength has not abated, and life seems as enjoyable to me as ever. But the happy thought is that God our heavenly Father rules and reigns and shall choose all our changes for us, for to His wisdom and love there is no limit. How sweet are the words, 'I have loved thee with an everlasting love,' 'As the Father hath loved Me, so have I loved you.' If we are His children we need not fear to trust our all in His hands. We need not desire to choose for ourselves in regard to the things of this life or the time when He shall call us to our heavenly home."

"That is a very sweet thought, father," she said. "What a care and anxiety it would be to us to have to choose changes for ourselves. How kind of the dear Lord Jesus to bid His disciples to take no thought—which you have explained to me means no care or anxiety—for the morrow—telling them that 'Sufficient unto the day is the evil thereof.'"

"Yes, and when we are troubled with cares and fear for the future, we may be sure that it is because we are only lacking in that faith that trusts all in His hands."

"Oh, I want that faith!" she exclaimed earnestly, though her voice was low and sweet. "Papa, pray for me that I may have it."

"I will, daughter. I already do," he said. "There is nothing I desire more strongly for you and all my dear children than that!"

They were silent for a moment, then she asked, "Where are we now, papa? And to what port are we bound as the first?"

"We are nearing Delaware Bay," he replied. "I expect to pass up it and the river to Philadelphia, where we will add Grandpa and Grandma Dinsmore to our party. Then we will come down and around the southern part of New Jersey and on up the eastern coast to Atlantic City. Rooms have been engaged for us at Haddon Hall, and there we propose staying for perhaps a fortnight. Then we are thinking of going on up the New England coast, perhaps as far as Bar Harbor in Maine."

"Oh, I like that plan," she said. "We have never yet visited Atlantic City, you know, and I have often wanted to do so."

"I shall be glad to give you that pleasure, my daughter," he said. "Now it is high time you were in bed and asleep. So bid me goodnight, and go."

Our travelers reached Philadelphia the next day, took on board Mr. and Mrs. Dinsmore, passed down the river and bay again, and up the Atlantic coast to the city of that same name, as the captain had planned.

They were charmed with their quarters in rooms near the sea—looking out directly upon it—with a private porch where they could sit and enjoy the breeze and an extended view of the ocean. They could watch the vessels pass and repass, outward bound or coming from distant ports to the harbors farther up the coast. Strolling along the broad plank walk, four miles in length and close to the sea, was another pleasure, as were also the driving down on the beach at low tide and the little excursions out to Longport and other adjacent villages.

Most of the days were spent in making these little trips — sometimes in carriages, others in the electric cars — and the evenings were spent in wandering by moonlight along the boardwalk.

There were various other places of innocent amusement, too, such as the Japanese garden and the piers, where seals and other curiosities were on exhibition.

They found their accomodations excellent and everything about the establishment homelike, neat, and refined. Their hostess was so agreeable, so charming, that their only regret was that they saw so little of her — so many were the calls upon her time and attention.

"She certainly must need an occasional rest," said Grandma Elsie one day, talking with Violet and the captain, "We must invite her to pay us a visit in our southern homes."

To that proposal both Captain Raymond and Violet gave an unqualified assent, saying that they would be pleased, indeed, to entertain her.

A fortnight was spent there most pleasantly, after which the *Dolphin* carried them up the coast to Bar Harbor.

The End

Invite little Elsie Dinsmore™ Doll Over to Play!

Breezy Point Treasures' Elsie Dinsmore™ Doll
brings Martha Finley's character to life in this
collectible eighteen-inch all-vinyl play doll
produced in conjunction with
Lloyd Middleton Dolls.

The Elsie Dinsmore™ Doll comes complete
with authentic Antebellum clothing and a
miniature Bible. This series of books emphasizes
traditional family values so your and your child's
character will be enriched as have
millions since the 1800's.